"We have to get  **too late."**

"Leave the safe house

Noel took her by the arm. "Let's go."

But when they stepped outside and saw a black SUV like the one that had smashed into them heading their way, he dragged her into the backyard.

"What are you doing?" she gasped.

"We did an exercise like this in Quantico. Trust me."

She followed him through the neighboring yard, sure her pounding heart would give away their position, then back to the garage. She joined him in the vehicle there and he pulled out. "So much for our lead. They heard us."

Of course they had. The past two days had been a nightmare that showed no sign of stopping. Yasmine watched in the side mirror as another SUV closed the gap between them.

Within seconds an arm snaked out the window on the passenger side, holding a gun.

For the first time since all of this had begun, a stark truth hit Yasmine right between the eyes.

They weren't going to make it.

Michelle Karl is an unabashed bibliophile and romantic suspense author. She lives in Canada with her husband and an assortment of critters, including a codependent cat and an opinionated parrot. When she's not reading and consuming copious amounts of coffee, she writes the stories she'd like to find in her "to be read" pile. She also loves animals, world music and eating the last piece of cheesecake.

Books by Michelle Karl

Love Inspired Suspense

Fatal Freeze
Unknown Enemy
Outside the Law

OUTSIDE THE LAW

MICHELLE KARL

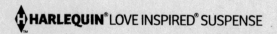

LOVE INSPIRED BOOKS

Recycling programs
for this product may
not exist in your area.

ISBN-13: 978-0-373-67814-3

Outside the Law

Copyright © 2017 by Faith Boughan

www.Harlequin.com

Printed in U.S.A.

Fear thou not; for I am with thee: be not dismayed;
for I am thy God: I will strengthen thee;
yea, I will help thee; yea, I will uphold thee
with the right hand of My righteousness.
—Isaiah 41:10

To my editor, Emily R, for her invaluable insight, and to my KV sisters, for their cherished encouragement.

ONE

"I'm going to be fine, Auntie Zee. Please stop worrying about me." Yasmine Browder hoisted her messenger bag higher on her shoulder and tucked her cell phone between her cheek and ear so she could reach back to pull her ponytail holder out of her hair. After having her hair up all day at the bakery, her scalp felt tight and in desperate need of relief. "I'm not lonely."

It was a partial truth, but she wanted to ease her aunt's anxieties, not add to them.

"I can't help but worry about you, honey." Her aunt's words were strained. "You've been back for only eight months and you work so hard, and now, with Daniel gone..."

Aunt Zara's voice trailed off, but Yasmine caught the unspoken meaning. She ignored it and slipped the hair elastic around her wrist. She pulled her sweater sleeves down, sneezing at the flour released from where it had become trapped in the fabric. She normally wore short-sleeved shirts to work, but the weather had cooled with the change of seasons—and besides, she often found herself chilled by the weather in western New York State. Especially after having returned here only about eight months ago from a ten-year stay overseas in the Kingdom of Amar, the desert-swathed country where most of her mother's family lived.

"I have to put in the work if I want Cinnamon Sunrise to thrive. Starting a small business is no easy feat." She'd come back to her hometown to live with her brother, but since his death several weeks ago, she'd begun wondering if she ever should have come back at all. He'd been happy to share his apartment with her, but now that she was on her own... well, Auntie Zee wasn't far off in her concerns. In dusty Amar, she'd never been alone, constantly surrounded by friends and family, whereas the prospect of entering the apartment tonight, knowing she'd spend the evening inside by herself watching television or reading—or, if she was being honest with herself, probably working on new recipes for the bakery's Thanksgiving menu—sounded less than appealing.

But what was her other option? Admit defeat to her aunt and listen to another lecture on why she was wasting her life running a bakery? Or phone a relative back in Amar, only to hear a different lecture about how she should move back there for good? That wasn't appealing, either, and besides, she loved Newherst. And New York State, despite the weather. She'd made a good life here in only eight months, and she cherished her childhood memories of this town.

"You're better than this, Yasmine. All that education and all that discipline you learned in the military, and you spend your days baking rolls. For what? You might as well go out and get married like your cousins. At least then—"

"I like what I do, auntie." Yasmine tried to maintain her composure as she trudged up the steps to her brother's fifth-floor apartment. The elevator would have been faster, sure, but staying health-conscious had become a priority since she started spending her days around breads, sweets and pastries. "And I'm surprised you're not more supportive. You remember that many of my recipes are based on your own wonderful creations, right? The people of Newherst adore your spiced flat-bread."

Her aunt grumbled unintelligibly as Yasmine reached the apartment door and dug in her bag for the keys.

"I'm home, auntie. I'll call you tomorrow, all right?"

"You'll come for dinner, is what you'll do. At six."

"The bakery closes at six. I'll come as soon as the doors are shut and locked." Yasmine found her keys in a side pocket and shook her head at the silliness of constantly losing the same item over and over each day, in the same bag, no less. She slipped the key into the lock.

"Fine." Her aunt went silent before releasing a heavy sigh. "I love you, honey. And I miss your brother."

"We all do, Auntie Zee. Love you, too, and see you tomorrow." She turned the door handle, slipped her phone into her messenger bag and paused.

Something felt wrong.

She pulled the door shut again and slipped the key out. When she'd turned the key, she hadn't heard a click, which meant that the door hadn't been locked after all. She clearly remembered locking the door that morning. The only other people with a key to this apartment were the building landlord and her aunt, and her aunt didn't drive.

Her throat grew tight and dry as she considered her options. Maybe it was a neighbor and the landlord had let the person in. Or maybe there'd been a utilities issue and someone had come inside to fix it, and nobody had locked up afterward.

She glanced down the hallway, seeing nothing else amiss.

"You're just being paranoid," she mumbled. "You're alone and jumpy since losing Daniel, and now look at you, talking to yourself. Get a grip before you give Auntie Zee more ammunition."

Taking a deep breath, Yasmine gripped the handle again and turned. She pushed open the door and lifted her messenger bag strap up to slip it off her shoulder. A click came from somewhere nearby, and she froze.

"Hello? Is somebody there?" *Stop it*, she thought. *There's nobody—*

Something zipped past her ear, splintering the door frame beside her. At the same instant, the two front windows shattered as black-clad bodies burst through them into the room, aiming large semiautomatic weapons at her.

As the next bullet zipped past her ear, she dropped to the floor and rolled out of the apartment, then sprang to her feet and sprinted down the hallway. Bullets tore through the wall beside her, ripping through her living room and bedroom. *Those are powerful guns.* She scolded herself for the thought. *Why are you analyzing their weapons at a time like this? Go, go, go!*

Her left knee began to sting, but despite knowing what that sting might mean, she kept moving. She'd taken a bullet before, during her time in the Amar military. She'd joined out of loyalty to her family's heritage and as a way to earn dual citizenship with both countries she considered home.

She reached the elevator and paused, but the thundering of boots behind her said she'd run out of time. It was back to the stairs.

She spun on her heel and slammed her body through the door into the stairwell. She felt air displacement as a bullet whipped past her shoulder. She gripped the hand rail and took the stairs three, four at a time, swinging her body around at each landing to gain precious seconds in her escape.

Of course, if whoever was shooting at her had left somebody outside to guard the exits, she'd be done for. And she'd never know why.

It doesn't make sense. Why are people shooting at me? And why shoot to kill instead of taking me into custody or as a hostage?

Had she done something or said something

political since returning from Amar? But that wouldn't make sense. Both countries were on the best of terms, especially since the recent discovery by an American professor of an ancient archaeological site in Amar had resulted in a boost in tourism and significant global press about the partnership between several universities there and here in the United States.

"I don't know anything," she said through gritted teeth. "What are you after?"

At the base of the stairs, she pressed her ear against the exit door, listening. She heard nothing unusual outside, but the pounding of heavy footfalls in the stairwell and the sudden ding of the elevator doors told her she'd run out of time to make a decision.

It was escape or die, which left her with only one real choice. She shoved the crash bar on the door, blinking against the descending sun's rays. The footfalls were growing closer and closer, and another gunshot told her that they weren't too concerned about ricochets in the metal stairwell—so they were very stupid, they wore full body armor or they were highly trained and incredibly accurate shots when presented with a normal target. Perhaps they hadn't accounted for her military training. Or maybe they had—maybe that's why there were so many of them.

Seeing no one outside waiting, Yasmine let the heavy metal door swing shut behind her as she sprinted toward the street. Several cars drove up and down the street on either side of the road, but she saw nothing unusual for this time of day...except the three black Suburbans parked in front of the apartment building. She crouched behind a steel waste container and peered around the corner, praying that nobody in the SUVs had been assigned to watch this edge of the building. When no one jumped out of the vehicles and ran toward her, she sent a quick prayer of thanks to God and tried to calm her racing thoughts.

At any second, men with guns would come bursting out of that stairwell door, and it wouldn't take them long to find her. She couldn't run back to the building to reach her car—the parking structure was on the other side, and if there were still men in the black SUVs, she'd never get there in one piece.

None of it made sense, but she'd have to figure out the whys later. If she survived.

She took a deep breath and counted to ten, exhaling slowly. She'd have to make a run for it down the street. She had to make it only one block before she'd reach a fairly busy street, where she should be able to get help and maybe flag down a ride to the police station. She plunged her hand into her bag and touched her phone, thinking to get a head start on a 911 phone call, but she'd run out of time—the side door burst open and five black-garbed men poured out and stood in a V-shaped formation, scanning the area. Even their faces were covered by shiny helmets and faceplates.

She swallowed hard, kicking herself for not moving seconds earlier. She'd taken too long to decide what to do next, but that didn't mean she was going to stay here and wait for a bullet to find her.

I don't know what's going on, Lord, but I'm going to trust that You have a way out for me. She closed her eyes and visualized the route she would take. *Three, two, one...*

Yasmine took off in a crouch from her hiding place, hoping the waste disposal bin would provide enough cover to distract the gunmen from seeing her right away. It didn't take long, though. While she didn't hear any shouts behind her, she felt air whoosh past her arm as she ran. They were still shooting, and they clearly didn't care if they hit anyone or anything else.

A car turned the corner at the end of the

block, and Yasmine's heart sank. She waved her arms, not caring if it made her a bigger target. "Turn around! Go back!" she shouted, hoping the driver would hear her, but he kept coming down the road. If he continued, he'd head right into the line of fire.

She veered off the sidewalk and into the street, heading directly toward the car. Even if the driver couldn't hear her or was trying to ignore her waving arms, there was no way he'd be able to avoid a person right in the middle of the street.

"Reverse! Call the police!" She reached the center of the street, but the car didn't slow down. She put on a burst of speed as more air displacement near her shoulder and waist told her that it was only a matter of seconds before the shooters had her directly in their sights.

And if the driver wouldn't stop, she'd force him to.

She ran straight toward the hood of the car and let herself be swiped by the side of the front bumper. The car screeched to a halt as she took the hit, tensing her body and rolling off to the side, collapsing on the opposite side of the hood.

Before the driver could open his door and jump out to ask questions, Yasmine reached up, grabbed the passenger door handle and threw open the door. Then she lunged inside, slammed the door shut and slid down in the seat so that she couldn't be seen through the windshield.

"There are men with guns coming this way," she said in a rush. "Reverse the car or we're both going to get shot."

As if in response, a bullet slammed against the windshield, sending a spider web of cracks spreading out from where it struck. Yasmine gaped. Why didn't it shatter?

Only then did she think to look at the driver of the car, who stared at her with an expression of utter disbelief. "Noel?" she said. "Noel Black?"

"Yasmine Browder?" He laughed, though his mouth hung open in shock. "What's going on here? Why are you in my car?"

Ping. Crack. More spider webs spread across the windshield. It didn't look like the thing could take many more hits.

"Can we do this later?" She pointed at the cracks. "Preferably while we're both still alive?"

"Right." He threw the car into Reverse, looked over his shoulder and stepped on the gas. The car shot to life. He backed down the street, turned the wheel and shifted gears to lunge forward and around the corner.

Yasmine released the breath she'd been holding and peeked through the rear window. "Thank you. If you don't mind, can I get a ride to the police station?"

Noel Black tried not to stare at the woman sitting in the passenger seat of his car. She looked terrified and trying very hard not to show it. After spending twenty weeks in the FBI Academy at Quantico for his special agent training, he'd seen that look on the faces of many of his classmates—and he'd probably worn it himself, to be honest—more than once in the time they'd all spent together. And those had only been Hogan's Alley training scenarios. He'd always hoped that look wouldn't appear on his own face the first time he tackled a real-life threatening situation, but he hadn't counted on receiving the shock of his life less than twenty-four hours after graduation.

He had a feeling he wasn't doing a very good job of hiding his surprise at seeing his childhood crush jump into his vehicle to avoid getting shot. *My poor car. Good thing I had her readied for duty last week.*

"You want to tell me what just happened?" he asked her, though what he really wanted to do was pull over and savor the moment of this reunion. How long had it been since he'd seen her—ten years? More? "Were those guys actually shooting at you?"

Yasmine shook her head and chewed on the edge of a fingernail as she stared through the back window. "Yes? No? I don't know. Look, Noel, I'm sorry to ask this of you, but I really do need to get to the police station. Actually, I should call 911 first, get them over there."

"Who were those guys?" He'd seen the black Suburbans at the end of the street and what appeared to be men in full black tactical gear—including facial coverings—down by the Willow Street apartment complex.

"I don't know."

"Were they after you?"

"It appears so, but I honestly don't know."

"Is there anything you *can* tell me?"

"No. Aren't you listening?" She twisted to look through the window again, then fell back against her seat with a huff. "If they shot up my reupholstered sofa, I'm going to be really upset."

Noel almost veered off the road at the inanity of her comment. "Masked men shooting at you for no reason, and you're worried about your sofa?"

"I'm probably in shock."

"You think?" Noel wanted to laugh, shout

at her and run into the fight all at the same time. Apparently a decade hadn't changed her one bit—she was still the same quirky girl he'd known from those days spent together watching cartoons and, later, preteen sitcoms when both of their moms had Bible study at her parents' apartment on Saturday mornings. The Browders' home had always smelled of cinnamon, nutmeg and honey. Didn't seem to matter what time of day or what time of year, middle of summer or dead of winter. In fact, he thought he could even smell it now.

The scent grew stronger as Yasmine shifted in her seat. Wait, was that scent coming from *her*? Noel swallowed a growing lump in his throat, fighting to suppress the surge of memory from those days when he'd accompanied his mother to her place just so he could sit near the pretty girl with the long, dark hair.

Beeping cut through the moment of memory. Yasmine had her phone out and was pressing buttons. She told the operator what had happened and mentioned that she was on the way to the Newherst Central Police Station. As she hung up and tucked the phone back into her bag, Noel considered how to broach the topic of…anything. Anything at all. What did you say to someone you hadn't seen for ten years who'd just jumped into your car to avoid gunfire?

He sent his mind into the past, trying to choose a safe topic. He could ask about her family or her time away. He couldn't remember exactly where she'd moved—he'd tried to look her up a few years back out of curiosity but couldn't find any social media profiles. Ask about what she was doing these days? It seemed too benign, especially considering the situation. They had armed gunmen to worry about, not a reunion to stage.

The police station parking lot came up quickly, and he pulled into a spot near the door. Yasmine fiddled with her seat belt, nervous fingers betraying her calm exterior. Best to take her mind off things with an easy, comforting question.

"So, how's your brother Daniel doing these days?"

Her fingers stopped moving. The silence that followed told him he'd made a huge mistake.

In one quick movement, she unlatched her seat belt and threw open the car door. She slipped out and leaned over to look at him with eyes of stone. "He died."

Noel's stomach and heart sank into his feet. Not Daniel. Yasmine hadn't been the only

Browder he'd shared Saturday mornings with. "Yasmine, I'm so sorry. I had no idea. Was it recent?"

"Three weeks ago." Her voice held no emotion as she pulled her body back from the car, feet and hips distancing themselves from him. "Freak workplace accident."

He wanted to ask where Daniel had worked, how it had happened, but the coldness in her expression told him that she'd already shut down. The woman had just been shot at, and now Noel had to go and bring her late brother into the conversation. Could he feel like any more of a jerk?

"I'll come in with you" is what he said instead. He slid out of his side of the car as Yasmine slammed the door. "I saw the trucks and some shooters, and ballistics may need to check my car over."

She shook her head. "It's okay. Don't feel like you owe me anything."

He circled his vehicle as she backed away. "You're the one who hurdled my car and used me as a getaway driver. Shouldn't I be saying that to you?"

The barest hint of a smile appeared. "Touché."

He came alongside her, and they strolled into the police station together. He reached for the door to hold it open for her, but she grabbed it first and held it open behind her for him. "I don't mean to pry," he said, "but do you know for sure no one else was in your apartment?"

She pursed her lips and sighed as they approached the reception desk. "I shared it with Daniel since coming back from Amar. And with him gone, it's just me. Shouldn't I be giving this info to law enforcement first? If you want to listen, fine, but—"

He felt a smirk crawl across the corner of his mouth as his right hand reached into his inner left jacket pocket. He touched the ID sleeve carrying his badge and FBI identification, which he still hadn't gotten used to carrying around—not that he'd had it for all that long. Less than a day, to be precise.

"What?" Yasmine's hands landed on her hips, the movement releasing more of that delicious scent of honey and cinnamon. "Since when is any of this something to smile about?"

He pulled out the ID holder and flashed his shiny new FBI shield for the first time since leaving Quantico, making sure Yasmine was the only one to see it. No need to alarm the local police or have them think he'd come to pull rank. They might not understand that he'd stumbled into the shooting scene by coincidence, and he'd rather have a handle on the situation before revealing his credentials.

Yasmine gaped at the badge, then looked from him to the receptionist and back at him. "What is that? Noel?"

He touched a finger to his lips. "Yasmine, I *am* law enforcement. And as much as I want to think that you returning from Amar, your brother's death and this attempt on your life are not related, let's not rule it out."

"But—" She stopped and crossed her arms. Looked at the floor with a frown and then back at him, her stony eyes reflecting a deep, fresh pain. When she spoke, her voice was almost a whisper. "Noel, there's something else you should know, something no one else believes me about because I don't have any proof."

He gripped her by the shoulders so she faced him straight on, but he let go just as quickly when he saw the surprise in her face. "You can trust me."

Whether she actually did or not, he couldn't tell, but he could tell she was keeping a secret that was eating her alive inside. He'd learned to identify that in training, so the knowledge was recent and clear.

She came to a decision, her eyes flicking

first to the pocket where he'd tucked his badge and then back at him. "I think Daniel might have been murdered."

TWO

Yasmine watched surprise blossom across Noel's face and immediately regretted her words. She shouldn't have said anything. She had no proof, nothing but a bad feeling about Daniel's death that had followed her for three weeks. Ever since the afternoon the phone call had come into the bakery as she served elderly Mrs. Notting her daily cinnamon bun and cup of sweet Turkish coffee.

She could still see the plate and cup hit the floor and shatter, mirroring Yasmine's heart in that very moment. She could feel the burn of the hot coffee where it had splashed back on her leg, leaving a round, red mark that stayed for a week after the incident. She remembered Mrs. Notting's surprised face at Yasmine's blunder, then the woman's leathery, wrinkled hands as they held Yasmine's flour-dusted palms and stroked her back as she knelt on the floor and wept.

"Forget it," she said, turning to the receptionist. "Hi, I'm the one who called in about the shooting at the Willow Street apartment complex?"

"Of course," said the receptionist, a willowy, forty-something woman with light brown skin and a name tag introducing her as Nia Hardy. "Officer Wayne is waiting to speak with you. One moment."

As the receptionist picked up her phone to call Officer Wayne to meet them, Noel touched Yasmine's arm, his brow furrowed.

"Please tell the police what you just told me."

She already had, weeks ago when she'd come to make a statement about Daniel's death, but the lack of proof hadn't gone over well. The officer she'd spoken to had taken her statement and done the equivalent of patting her on the hand and sending her away. "Forget it."

"Yasmine, I'm serious."

"I said, forget it."

"Is that a no?"

"Ah, Miss Browder." Yasmine's heart sank as Officer Wayne rounded the corner. This was the same officer who'd taken her statement about Daniel. He now gave her a look akin to mild suspicion. "What have you come to see us about today? Not more conspiracy theories, I hope."

Yasmine nearly lunged at the man, but Noel's arm shot out to grasp the receptionist's countertop, blocking her way. Part of her wanted to shove through and give the officer a stern talking-to, but another part felt grateful for Noel's intervention before she made a bad situation worse.

"Miss Browder was attacked in her home by armed gunmen," Noel explained. "I happened to be driving by and brought her to safety."

Officer Wayne eyed Noel warily as though uncertain whether to trust anyone associated with her. The men were silent as they sized each other up, until finally Officer Wayne sighed, dropped his shoulders and waved them forward.

"Right. Come down to the desk so I can take your statements."

Fifteen minutes later, she stormed out of the station with Noel on her heels, though he was obviously less incensed. They'd given their statements to Officer Wayne, who'd refused to tell her anything about what the dispatched police had found when they'd arrived at her presumably shot-to-pieces apartment.

"He thinks it's gang violence, Noel." She glared at him as he came alongside her. "Gang violence!"

"There *is* a precedent for groups from Buffalo extending their reach into small towns."

"Do you really think that my apartment was shot up randomly? Three weeks after my brother— You know what? Forget it." She blinked away hot tears behind her anger lest he, too, think that she was overreacting. She stalked away from Noel, from Officer Wayne and everyone else who looked at her like she'd gone crazy.

The worst of it was, if she'd been in their shoes, she'd probably have thought the exact same thing about her claims and accusations. No proof, no evidence, no reason to suspect anything other than the obvious answer.

"How are you planning to get home?" Noel quickened his pace to get in front of her as they reached the parking lot. "Do you have someone who can give you a ride?"

She stopped walking and stared at the lot. Right. She hadn't driven here, and Noel's car was needed as evidence for ballistics. He'd handed over his car keys to Officer Wayne.

"And do you have someplace to stay tonight?" he continued. "Somewhere to go since your apartment is off-limits?"

It was a lot of questions from a man she hadn't seen in ten years and who didn't even live here anymore. They might have been friends once, and she might have had a childish crush on him a decade ago, but as grateful as she was that he'd appeared in her street at just the right time and had pursued a law enforcement career, she'd had enough of surprises and other people for one day.

"I'm going to walk down the street and get something to eat, since apparently I'm in no danger and am simply an incidental victim of gang violence. It's been a long day, and I'd like to get off my feet. I'll figure out the rest as I go."

"Want company?"

"Not particularly." She shoved her hands in her pockets, squeezing her arms to her sides.

"Okay." He looked disappointed but didn't press her. "Can I at least give you my phone number while I'm here? In case you run into more trouble, or if you can't find a place to stay? I'm sure my parents would put you up in the spare room."

"Aren't you staying in the spare room?"

"Not if you need it. I can go elsewhere."

He stopped walking, and she noticed only

after she'd taken several steps ahead. Was he really going to give up that easily? The sincerity on his face made her feel bad for rejecting his company. After all, he'd driven her here and gotten his car shot up by the guys who'd come after her.

She'd also be lying to herself if she said she wasn't curious about what he'd been up to since she'd boarded the plane for Amar a decade ago. Maybe a little company wouldn't be too bad, at least for dinner. It didn't have to mean anything. *Keep telling yourself that, Yasmine.*

Her heart did a little flip when she looked back at him. He'd grown into his frame well. The last time she'd seen him, he was all arms and legs, with spiky blond hair and front teeth that only a mama rabbit would love. Now his shoulders were broad and strong, and he'd filled out his features. His stance radiated confidence, and if she hadn't known he'd gone into law enforcement, she'd have guessed at some kind of work that required both strength and mental fortitude. He hadn't flinched when she'd given the order to drive as bullets peppered his car's windshield. Quite a different Noel from the boy she'd known who'd refused to talk to her for months after he'd confessed his crush on her when she was nine and he, eleven.

She'd developed feelings for him far too late to do anything about it—they'd been like ships passing in the night, because by the time she'd gathered the courage to tell him about her girlish crush at fourteen years old, her parents had already planned to whisk the family off to be with her ill grandmother before she passed away, and the trip became a move. Besides, at the time, she'd thought he probably didn't care for her anymore. Not as more than a friend, anyway, since he always seemed to be holding hands with one girl or another in the hallways at school.

Surely he'd gotten married and had several children by now. She couldn't see his ring finger from where she stood, but the thought of allowing a married Noel Black to eat dinner with her and catch up seemed less threatening than it initially had.

"Look, I didn't mean to sound rash," she said. "There's a little Mediterranean restaurant up the road, a five-minute walk. I'd like to hear what you've been up to and how you got that flashy new accessory."

He nodded and rejoined her. They walked more or less in silence toward the restaurant,

Yasmine leading the way. After a few minutes, Noel broke the stalemate.

"Yasmine, what you said about Daniel—"

"Can we not? Not right now. Not here."

"Sure, sure."

The silence resumed until they neared the intersection where the little restaurant was located. They stood waiting for the walk signal, but when the light turned green, one of the cars at the intersection backfired. Yasmine gasped and ducked out of instinct. Her cheeks immediately warmed as she realized her blunder, seeing an antique-looking red convertible sputter through the intersection and down the road.

She accepted Noel's outstretched hand to help her back to her feet, but resented the raised eyebrow he turned on her.

"Can you blame me?" she muttered before hoofing it across the street. As if she didn't have enough to deal with today, without getting jumpy at every loud noise. She pulled open the door to the Mediterranean restaurant and held up two fingers for the hostess. The young woman pulled two menus from a pile at the host stand and seated Yasmine and Noel in a booth by the front window.

Yasmine flipped open the menu but closed

it immediately. She knew what she wanted to eat. Something familiar and comforting. Today was not the day to take risks.

"What's good here?" Noel perused the menu with feigned interest. Yasmine could tell that he wasn't paying full attention. His frequent glances at her said that he had questions to ask, but he hoped she'd answer them without him saying a word.

She tried to pretend she didn't notice and gazed out the window at the passing cars. "The moussaka here is fantastic. Better than my aunt's version, but don't tell her."

"Moose-what? What's in that, eggplant?" He tapped the plastic-covered menu and sighed. "I have to admit, I'm relieved that I was the one driving down your street this afternoon. I was on my way to the bank on the other side of town and decided to take a shortcut down Willow. If I hadn't come along when I did…"

His voice trailed off, and she felt his eyes bore into her. She wanted to eat and find a place to sleep. Her aunt would take her in without question—well, maybe a few questions—but she'd also want to talk about Daniel. And there'd be worry and fussing and phone calls overseas. Yasmine just wanted a place to lie down and close her eyes. Her 5:00 a.m. start at the bakery would come soon enough, as it always did.

"Yasmine?"

Her attention snapped back to him at the sudden tension in his voice. His posture had gone rigid, and he stared at a spot below her clavicle. She tried to follow his gaze.

"Don't!" he exclaimed.

Alarm sliced through her stomach, and she hardly dared to breathe. She saw the panic in his eyes, panic that he'd obviously been trained to bury. "What is it?"

His throat tightened, and she looked anyway as he took a sharp breath. She froze as her eyes locked on the red dot that wavered directly over her heart.

A sniper outside had pinned her in his crosshairs.

Noel tried to clamp down on the panic. This was real life. Not a training exercise. Less than twenty-four hours out of Quantico and the woman across the table from him had a sniper ready to end her life at any moment.

What was the right move in this situation? *You're sitting here thinking, and that shot could kill her before you blink.*

"Get down!" he shouted. He waited until he saw her move before launching himself sideways.

Glass shattered around them, and the thud of bullets hitting the back of the booth told Noel she'd gotten out of the way just in time. She lay sprawled on the floor as screams erupted inside the restaurant, patrons leaping from their seats to head to the back of the room. He reached for Yasmine's arm, and she crawled toward him.

"Everyone okay?" he called into the restaurant. "Has anyone been hurt? Check your neighbor!" The patrons scrambled to check limbs and look each other over, sending thumbs up his way to indicate they were all right. With no immediate injuries to handle, he turned his attention back to Yasmine.

"You all right?" The way she favored her left knee looked worrisome.

"I'm fine," she said. She crouched next to him behind the next set of booth seats. "Shouldn't we get out of here?"

"Not until I know it's safe." He touched the gun holstered on his side, reminding himself it was there if he needed it. He peered around the corner of the booth, scanning for any unusual movement across the street, but at seven o'clock, the descending twilight made it difficult to see anything out of place. Plenty of cars zoomed through the intersection just outside the front door, oblivious to the goings-on inside the restaurant.

"How will you know that?" Yasmine sounded impatient. "I feel like a sitting duck here. We should move."

"No. We wait for the police."

"Whoever shot at me will be gone by then. If it's a sniper, he won't have had time to set up again and will be on the move. We can spot him. It's not like it's easy to disguise a sniper rifle. Let's go!"

Noel stared at Yasmine, whose entire body seemed to tremble with the need to get up and move. "No. We let the police handle it." He pulled out his phone and began to call the direct line to the station, but a growl of frustration stopped him short.

The sharpness of Yasmine's glare could have cut him in two. "I thought you *were* the police now."

"In a manner of speaking, but this isn't my jurisdiction."

"Sounds like an excuse. I'm not going to cower here. This is the second attempt on my life today, and that shooter might have information about why it's happening."

She had a compelling argument. But it

seemed foolhardy to run into danger, though it was still early evening and the streets crowded. A sniper would certainly be in retreat, and she made a good point about being able to spot him.

He ran a hand across his face and groaned. "I'm going to regret this, aren't I?"

"Of course not. Make the call on the way if you have to. Let's go." Without waiting for his assent, she clapped him on the shoulder and ran in a crouch past the remaining front windows. When she reached the door, she scanned the roofs of the nearby buildings, then took off outside. Noel scrambled after her, trying not to show the shock he felt at her audacity. What made her think she could take on a sniper?

For that matter, how had she gotten away from all those gunmen who'd come after her less than two hours ago at her apartment building? And how was she keeping her cool so well? There was more to Yasmine Browder than he remembered. Something had happened to turn his delicate and shy but sarcastic childhood friend into a woman of strength and confidence.

When he stepped out of the restaurant, he saw Yasmine weaving between people on the sidewalk, heading away from the police station. He was loath to leave the crime scene, but there were many eyewitnesses inside who could explain what they'd seen. And when the police finally caught up with him and Yasmine…well, flashing the shield was inevitable at this point.

"Black!" she called him, gesturing while looking down the street. "This way." He noticed she took care to position herself near garbage cans and mailboxes along the block as she went. She'd learned how to seek cover, how to make herself less of a target. And she claimed not to know anything about these people after her? Believing that was becoming more and more difficult.

He caught up to her. "Don't run off like that. If we're going to find this guy, we need to stick together."

"Yeah, well, if I hadn't waited for your go-ahead, I'd have him already. The delay cost us. He's probably long gone." Her glance at him was not friendly. "I thought Feds were trained to protect the public from danger, not sit around and wait for local PD to think about maybe doing something."

He felt his hackles rise at the insult. "Listen, Yasmine, I don't know what makes you think you can—"

"There!" She pointed down the sidewalk,

two blocks away. A man with a large black backpack had just crossed the street. There was nothing otherwise incriminating about him, but the moment Noel saw the man's profile, his newly honed instincts kicked in.

There was something off about that guy, and Yasmine had found him before Noel did. Some new Fed he was turning out to be.

"Come on, Black." Yasmine began walking quickly down the sidewalk. Noel followed close behind, keeping one hand on his sidearm, but at this distance he noticed again that she favored her left leg. It didn't seem to slow her down, though, and they started to gain on the man.

Noel tried to memorize a description of the individual as they drew closer. Dark clothing, close-cut dark hair, small ears, sharp nose. The backpack was black and had no logo, and if a shooter had the dexterity to take a shot and disassemble his weapon quickly, it would fit inside the main compartment of the bag.

The man approached the next intersection as the light turned red. Noel and Yasmine were only half a block away. Noel gripped the handle of his sidearm, ready to act. They'd reach the man in a matter of seconds.

The man looked to his left and right as he waited. And then over his shoulder. He locked eyes with Noel and, in an instant, shifted from person of interest to suspect.

The man took off, dodging oncoming cars as he sprinted across the road. Horns blared and onlookers shouted in surprise, and of course Yasmine was right behind, taking advantage of the braking cars to weave the same path. Adrenaline shot through Noel's system as he drew his gun and raced after both of them.

"Stop, FBI!" His shout only spurred the suspect on. In a burst of speed, the man continued down the sidewalk, pushing people out of the way. Noel ached to stop and help them, to make sure they were okay, but if the runner was also the shooter, he'd do far greater good by catching the man and bringing him in.

"This way," Yasmine said suddenly, grabbing Noel's arm and pulling him off course.

"What are you doing?" Noel growled at her, but their momentum had already been redirected as she led them down an alley behind a building. Their path, unimpeded by passersby or sidewalk signage, brought them to the other side of the block. They emerged from the alley moments before the suspect turned the corner, looking back over his shoulder for his pursuers.

With practiced efficiency, Yasmine grabbed

the man's shoulder and pushed him to the ground, twisting his arm behind his back. He tried to rise, but Yasmine managed to grip his other arm and hold them both in place.

"Get off!" The man shouted. "I've done nothing wrong!"

"I'll be the judge of that," Noel said, training his gun on the struggling suspect. He really needed to find out how Yasmine had learned that move, too. He leaned over and carefully, with Yasmine's help, pulled off the man's backpack. The man groaned in pain as Yasmine held him in place. "I don't want to hurt you, sir, but I am armed and authorized to use lethal force if necessary."

"Get her off me, man. She's going to break my arm."

"You'll be fine," Yasmine muttered. "It'll just hurt for a few days."

But the last thing Noel needed on his first day as an official special agent was an assault charge on his hands. He kept his firearm trained on the man and waved the backpack. "Yasmine, I'm throwing this to you. Release his arms. He's not going anywhere. Right?"

"Whatever," muttered the man.

Yasmine released her hold, and Noel tossed her the backpack. She unzipped it and looked inside, then nodded at him. The gun was there. They had the sniper.

"Who sent you?" Yasmine looked angry enough to rival any FBI interrogator. "Why are you shooting at me? Who shot up my apartment?"

The man on the ground flipped onto his back, looked up at her and grinned. His jaw tensed as though he'd bitten down on something, and a shiver ran down Noel's spine. Something about this wasn't right...

Suddenly the man's eyes rolled up, and he began to convulse.

"Yasmine, get back!" Noel reached for her and pulled her next to him, stepping away from the suspect.

Foam rose from between the man's lips as he shook. Then, as quickly as it started, it was over. The man didn't move. His eyes were open and glazed, lifeless. Horror seeped into Noel's insides as he considered the meaning of the man's seizure. He stepped up to the body and knelt, pressing his fingers against the side of the man's throat. No pulse.

"What just happened?" Yasmine stared at the man on the ground. "We had him. We had him and he was going to tell me why I've been used for target practice today."

Noel shook his head and stepped back. "No, he wasn't."

Yasmine regarded him with wide eyes. He didn't want to have to tell her this, to explain that he suspected something very big was going on and that she had to know why. She had to be hiding information. No one got targeted twice in one day.

Even fewer had their assailants commit suicide upon capture.

"Yasmine?" He tried to keep his voice level, for her sake. It had taken only seconds for this seemingly fearless person before him to go from warrior to worried young woman.

"What?" Her hands shook as she held the backpack, and he wished he knew what thoughts swirled through her head.

"You said when we were in the police station that you suspect your brother's death wasn't an accident. Regardless of what Officer Wayne believes, I think we need to sit down so you can tell me why. Because if it's true, seems like the death of one Browder wasn't enough. Somebody's eager to make sure you're out of the picture, too. It's time to tell me what you know."

THREE

Yasmine's hands trembled as she waited in the police station for Noel. She held a lukewarm cup of coffee that she'd accepted more for the warmth radiating from the beverage than anything else. She felt cold, so very cold, and her stomach hurt. Whether from lack of food or the strain of the day, she didn't know. Did it matter?

She rubbed the side of her left knee, feeling for the place a bullet had grazed her as she ran through the apartment building only hours before. It still stung, but it hadn't bled too much, and going to the hospital to stitch it up seemed a needless waste of time. It would heal if only she stopped running away from shooters and watching them die in front of her.

It didn't make sense. Why would anyone want to kill her? And why would the shooter, once caught, commit suicide to avoid talking? The only thing she could figure was that this whole day had to be a case of mistaken identity.

Noel had wanted her to talk immediately about Daniel's death, but the police had arrived on-scene—thankfully Officer Wayne hadn't been among them—and they'd had to give those reports first. Besides, she felt a little silly for having blurted out her suspicion to him earlier. She'd been pumped up with adrenaline after escaping the shooters in her apartment, not to mention unexpectedly seeing Noel again after ten years. When it came right down to it, her hunch about Daniel's death was just that—a hunch. She had no proof, nothing concrete but a knowledge that Daniel was an exceptionally careful worker and that the routine investigation into the work accident that claimed his life had been wrapped up in less than forty-eight hours. Packaged up with a little bow and presented in a press release in the local paper. Unfortunate tragedy, they'd said. Completely preventable, if only Daniel had taken the correct precautions during his shift. Yasmine couldn't believe that her brother, the safety fanatic, would have done anything to endanger himself or others.

And it only added to her uncertainty about the whole thing that just a few days before,

Daniel had said something she wished she'd paid more attention to at the time.

"I think I stumbled across something at work today," he'd said as she rushed to pack herself a lunch at quarter to five in the morning. Daniel wasn't usually up so early, but sometimes he had trouble sleeping and spent time online playing games or working on lesson plans for the online engineering courses he occasionally taught through a local adult education center. She'd hardly paid attention to him as he spoke to her that day. "I was waiting in the boss's office to present him with a briefing, and I saw one of the reports I'd filed a week earlier. It didn't look right."

"Mmm-hmm," she'd said, barely giving him a second glance. "Not right, how?"

"The numbers on the inspection sheet…I didn't get much of a chance to take it all in before Clarke returned to the office. We got caught up in conversation, so I forgot about it. But now that I think back, it can't have been right. Those numbers were not the same."

"You probably missed the date or something," she'd said. "Maybe you were looking at an old report. You said yourself that you didn't get much chance to take it all in."

Daniel had rubbed his eyes and sighed. "That's true."

"So why are you losing sleep over it? And if you're worried about a problem, you should talk to your boss about it, not me." She'd closed her lunch sack and tucked it into the colorful patchwork messenger bag she used as a purse, a gift from one of her Amaran cousins. "He might even be grateful—if there is a problem, he might be too busy to have spotted it. You might be doing the place a favor."

He'd nodded, but even when he agreed with her, his voice sounded uncertain. "Yeah. Maybe. Thanks, sis. Hope you don't burn anything today." He'd playfully punched her in the shoulder and she'd punched him back. "Bring me home a cinnamon roll or some baklava."

"You don't need any more sweets, Daniel." She'd given him an appraising eye, just like their mother used to do when either of them took a second helping of dessert, and they'd both laughed. He'd waved her off and she'd headed to work, forgetting about the conversation moments after closing the apartment door.

Days later, he was dead. And it wasn't until a week after the funeral that she'd recalled their conversation and realized that maybe—just maybe—she'd told him to do the very thing that had gotten him killed.

It was supposition. Pure conjecture. But still, she couldn't shake the awful feeling that somehow, Daniel might actually have seen something he wasn't supposed to. And she'd told him to tell his boss about it.

The timing all seemed a little too convenient.

On the other hand, without proof or anything to substantiate her feelings, nobody had any reason to take her seriously. Especially not Noel, the big FBI agent.

"Ready to go?" Noel crossed the station toward her, tossing a set of keys up and catching them as he moved. Officer Wayne came with him, his expression flat and unreadable. "I went through your old reports with Wayne, and we're set to go."

"You have your car back?" Yasmine made a point of not looking in the officer's direction, but that meant she needed to focus on Noel—and it was hard not to notice once again that the physique of her childhood friend had changed considerably in the past decade. He'd been such a scrawny thing back in the day. It was going to take some getting used to, seeing him filled out and carrying himself with the utmost confidence. What on earth had inspired timid Noel Black to enter the FBI, anyway? She also hadn't yet had the chance to ask him about his family. What a day this was turning out to be.

"No." Noel sighed. "Not yet. But Officer Wayne here knows a guy and had him bring over a car for us."

"Us?" Yasmine narrowed her eyes at him.

Noel cleared his throat and clutched the keys as they dropped once more into his hand. "Yes, us. I'm taking you to my parents' place. You'll be safe there. You can't go back to your apartment tonight, and I'm sure my mom would love to see you."

Yasmine almost laughed. "I've seen your mom more than you probably have, Noel. I own a bakery here in town, and she's come in a few times."

He raised an eyebrow at her, and she was flooded with the memory of Noel and Daniel as they joked together while playing board games. What was that old one, *Mastermind*? They loved to play that, though they always seemed to make up their own rules. "I guess she wouldn't have mentioned I went to Quantico, since I didn't even tell her at first. I wanted to make sure I could hack it, since the drop-out and dismissal rate is fairly high."

"She did mention once that you'd gone through police training a few years ago or something like that."

Noel grimaced at her words but didn't elaborate. "Yeah. Something like that."

"FBI and Police Academy," Officer Wayne muttered. "That explains it."

"Anyway, I can stay with my aunt." She didn't want to, really didn't want to. "There's no point in me putting your mom out, especially not when I have family here in town. Officer, are you sure I can't go back to my apartment and pick up a few things?"

Officer Wayne frowned. "No."

"Maybe by tomorrow?" Noel glanced at Officer Wayne, who only shrugged. Was that remorse she saw on Wayne's face? Had he finally realized that Yasmine hadn't been overreacting all this time? "I wouldn't recommend going back by yourself," Noel said.

"Not until we've got a better handle on what's happening here." Officer Wayne looked at the floor for a moment before training his steely gaze on her. "We're going to find out who did this to you and why."

She swallowed down a sarcastic retort about the police's refusal to take her earlier suspicions seriously. "So you've been reexamining the reports I've given to date?" When Officer Wayne grunted in the affirmative, she stood and pulled out her cell phone. "Good. You know how to reach me if there are any further questions. I'll have my aunt come and get me."

Noel shook his head and backed toward the exit. "No way. It's been ten years, Browder. I'm not letting you get away that easily, not when we have a whole fifteen minutes to catch up on the way to your aunt's place. Plus, this way I can keep an eye on you. We don't know if the shooter was acting alone or if the person who sent him is anywhere nearby. The shooting at your apartment may or may not be related, and whether the guys who shot up your apartment were gang members or not, I'll feel better personally seeing you safely to your aunt's place. Did you want to call and let her know you're coming?"

"I'm not getting out of this, am I?"

"Nope." Noel jingled the keys and waved one hand to the retreating Officer Wayne. "Come on. We have some catching up to do. It'll take your mind off the events of the day."

Not likely. She followed him to the car and made a quick phone call to Auntie Zee, who was ecstatic to hear that she was coming over—less so to hear that she'd been involved in the shootings reported on the news that day. Yasmine left out most of the details, just giving her aunt enough to understand why Yasmine would be coming over for the night.

She climbed into the car as Noel got himself oriented to the new vehicle. The concentration on his face reminded her of the times they'd spent trying to figure out the newspaper crossword puzzles together, or the look on his face during a particularly trying round of *Scrabble*. A sudden pang of longing struck her—a longing for the past, for how close they'd been, for how Noel had treated her like she was a precious jewel. She'd been too young and hadn't appreciated it until it was too late.

"So—" They both spoke at the same time, bringing an extra layer of awkwardness to the moment. Noel laughed nervously and started the car.

"You first," Yasmine said. "And sorry again about getting your car shot to bits."

"You'll have to remind me how to get to your aunt's place. And it's not your fault my car got shot up," Noel said with a shrug. The vehicle reversed out of the parking lot, and he turned onto the main street. "I'm blaming the guys who did it, and when the police catch them, you'd better believe that they'll be paying."

"The police? You're not helping?"

He shook his head. "There's nothing in the shootings that places this within federal jurisdiction. So far a building and a restaurant have been shot up while you were inside, but I can't take over because of that. I realize that sounds ridiculous, but the FBI works differently in reality than in movies."

"We caught the restaurant shooter. And he killed himself. Can't you step in and look for the guys at my apartment now?"

"Doesn't matter. Until there's a cause of death determined for sure, and only if that gets passed up the chain, there's nothing I can do. The FBI isn't exactly called in for suicides, Mina."

Yasmine stared at the man beside her. She hadn't heard anyone call her that in…well, ten years. "*Mina.* You remembered."

He glanced sideways at her with a half smile. "Of course I remember. It's been a while, but we're not strangers."

Warmth and regret flooded Yasmine's heart, but she shoved it aside just as quickly. So what if he'd grown up to be a handsome man? She had no place thinking of him as anything other than a childhood friend. And besides, he'd only be in her life for a day or two at most. She didn't know much about how the FBI worked, but she did know that they tended to send people all over the country.

There was no way Noel had been assigned to their little town in western New York.

"Turn left at the next stoplight," she said. "And you're right, but ten years is a long time not to speak to someone, Noel. We're strangers in almost every way at this point."

She'd meant it to be a lighthearted comment, but it came out sounding cold.

"You're right. It *is* a long time." His voice had gone flat, emotionless.

"That's not what I meant. It's more like, what have you been up to? Are you married, have kids? Do you still like to watch Saturday morning cartoons? I'm curious. It's like having a big brother who goes away to school whom you don't get to see until after graduation."

"Big brother, huh?" He remained rigid, not looking at her. "But I'm not the one who went away, Yasmine. I'm not the one who disappeared for ten years without so much as a goodbye."

Yasmine's heart sank toward her shoes. This wasn't how she'd imagined their reunion would be, not that she ever truly entertained the notion that they'd see each other again.

And she'd meant to look him up once she returned to the United States. She really had, but getting the bakery up and running took first priority, and helping Daniel manage the apartment, plus volunteering on her church's outreach committee...well, connecting with old friends had taken a backseat.

It wasn't like Noel had reached out to her, either. Surely his mother had mentioned running into her at the bakery. And he was FBI now, so it was hard to believe that he couldn't have found her if he'd really searched.

So, why did she feel so guilty?

"Look, I didn't mean to leave without saying goodbye." Her voice was so soft, she wondered for a moment if she'd spoken out loud or merely thought the apology. "I considered you my best friend. Even after I acted like a jerk and laughed at your declaration."

Noel chuckled, and she heard the ache behind it. The memory clearly remained as fresh and painful for him as it did for her, as if it had happened yesterday. "I should have known better. We were friends, that's all. You'd never shown interest in me that way, and I was an awkward kid. If I'd had any smarts about girls, I'd have been much smoother to ensure that by the time I said something, you'd have liked me back."

"Give yourself a little credit, at least. That was a very brave thing to do."

"I don't know about that." She saw his

hands tighten around the steering wheel. "Sometimes I wish I hadn't said anything at all."

Yasmine sighed and leaned her head against the window. "I'm glad you did. I only wish I'd clued in sooner, because by the time I tried to tell you the same thing, you already had a girlfriend from school. Do you remember that?"

Noel scratched his chin, thinking. "Actually, no. You tried to tell me you had a crush on me?"

She laughed softly. "Figures. Yes, it was the last time we saw each other. Our moms had Bible study group and you hadn't come for a while, but that day you came and you brought Suzanna. Cute blonde, thinner than me. Great legs—I think she ran track at school? Anyway, I poured sparkling apple juice for all of us and then went to the freezer for a package of frozen pitas to make a snack. You followed me and asked if you could help with anything. I was so startled that you'd do that—you were usually clueless about that kind of thing."

"How do you remember all this?" Noel shook his head in disbelief. "I remember that I came over that day and there was a girl with me, but I can barely recall what she looked like, let alone what happened."

Yasmine groaned. "Boys! Go figure! It was literally that moment that I tried to tell you I finally had a crush on you, too. But I tried to be, you know, kinda subtle about it because I was afraid that Suzanna would overhear."

"Uh, I think you were far too subtle, because I honestly don't remember that."

"Turn right up here. And of course you don't." She twisted in her seat to face him, though he kept his eyes on the road. "I don't remember what you said, but it was something hurtful. I know it wasn't meant to be and you'd misunderstood me, but it felt like a rejection all the same. The next day, my aunt and mom explained that we were going to visit family in Amar because my grandmother had fallen ill."

"But you never came back. You're telling me you were supposed to be there only for a visit?"

She swallowed the urge to cut off her story, to give him a patronizing answer and not relive the next part of the tale. But she'd already started telling it, and it would be cruel to back down now. "I promise this is the truth, Noel. I didn't mean to disappear without a word, but the illness was sudden, and we had to leave quickly. I'd never met my grandmother before, and my mom wanted me to have that chance before she passed. When we arrived, her condition had worsened, and it was clear she wouldn't be with us much longer, so mom wanted to stay and be with her to the end. My schoolwork for the rest of the year was done through mail and email, and by the time my grandmother went to be with Jesus, we were so engrained with my extended family and my mother was so heartbroken by the loss of her mother that we stayed. My dad was still alive at the time and able to work remotely, so one week blended into the next, and the next thing I knew..."

"Ten years had passed," Noel murmured. "That still doesn't explain why you didn't contact me. Daniel sent a few letters. Did you know that? I didn't see him after he moved back to the States, but he called me once to see how I was doing."

"Sounds like Daniel," Yasmine said. Her words hitched, a lump forming in her throat. "I really miss him."

"Me, too." She wasn't the only one having difficulty—she heard Noel's words grow thick with emotion. "I wish I'd had a chance to say goodbye. Or anything, really."

Silence descended once again as the memory of Daniel washed over them. She heard the hitch of Noel's breath and wished that they weren't driving so she could reach out to him, take back the way she'd snapped at him earlier when he'd only tried to help. He *had* helped, and generously so. Then again, what made her think that he'd find comfort in her?

"It's the third house on the right up here, the yellow one with lavender flowers in front."

Noel pulled into her aunt's driveway, and Yasmine couldn't help but feel regretful that their conversation had ended on such a low note—but at the same time, she didn't know what to say to make it better.

"Breakfast tomorrow?"

She whipped her head around, certain she'd heard him wrong. "Breakfast? Together?" He laughed, and she felt a rush of warmth to her cheeks. Of course he didn't know what a ludicrous suggestion that was. "You realize I have to be at the bakery by five in the morning to get everything ready for the day, right? We'd have to eat at four fifteen, four thirty at the latest."

His smile slipped at the mention of a four o'clock start to the day. "That's... You do that every day? Do you have to?" She raised one eyebrow at him, and he lifted his palms in defeat. "Okay, okay. How about this? I'll drive you to work. We can grab coffee and a breakfast sandwich on the way, and we can talk in the car. I'm heading that direction back to the station tomorrow anyway. Officer Wayne started to see reason and agreed with me that where there's a shooter who takes his own life, the boss can't be far behind. Just in case there's still a danger to you, I'm going to be hanging around outside your aunt's place tonight. An officer on patrol might come spell me for a bit if I can convince Captain Simcoe, but you won't be alone. I don't think we can be too careful after today's events."

She shook her head. "I appreciate it, but you don't have to do that."

"I want to, and you can't talk me out of it. I'll be ready to go at quarter to five tomorrow, okay?"

Yasmine wanted to yell that the police should really be the ones setting a watch for her when Daniel's killer roamed free, that Noel didn't need to exhaust himself on her behalf, but at least it would be a start. Once Officer Wayne finished examining her reports and corroborated them with the events of today—and accepted that even an FBI agent believed that something dangerous was happening—he'd have to believe her. Maybe even send the case up to the captain, who held the power to launch a real investigation.

In the meantime, Noel driving her to work

would be, well, nice. He didn't think she was crazy, and she found herself almost looking forward to spending a little more time together. Their conversations had all been cut too short.

"Fine, but four thirty is a better time. I don't want to stop for any of those mass-produced chain restaurant pastries. Mine are much tastier. Actually—" She paused, her legs dangling out the door. "We'll go right to the store. You can sit behind the counter as I prep. I'll make breakfast. Tomorrow is salted caramel cinnamon roll and blueberry lavender scone day."

Noel's smile returned, and Yasmine felt her expression mirror his in spite of herself. "Now *that* will be worth waiting here through the night for."

He waved as she shut the door and walked up the front steps to her aunt's house. As she stepped inside, she looked back over her shoulder at the childhood friend who waited to ensure she made it safely. She waved back at him as she crossed the threshold, then closed the door as he parked across the street.

Only then did it occur to her that her heart was beating rapidly, her palms warm and her cheeks flushed. And as much as she didn't want to admit it, the truth was impossible to deny—her reaction had nothing to do with all the bullets that had flown at her today, and everything to do with the handsome FBI agent whose car she'd leaped inside of only hours before.

Noel's cell phone alarm woke him at four thirty-two the following morning. He waved at the police cruiser that had pulled up a few hours ago to allow Noel to get a bit of rest. He didn't want his ability to protect Yasmine compromised by exhaustion, and it hadn't been difficult to convince the police captain last night to send some officers over to help out—especially after he played the FBI card. The police cruiser revved up and pulled away as Noel rubbed the sleep from his eyes. Despite his best efforts to rest, he'd spent most of the past few hours fidgety and unable to stop the events of the day from playing out over and over again in his mind. One thing was certain: they needed to talk more about Yasmine's suspicions surrounding Daniel's death. Despite the police's dismissal of her claims, he wanted to hear the story straight from Yasmine herself.

He unclipped his seat belt to head up to the house and collect her, but she slipped outside just as he disengaged the vehicle locks. She closed the door behind her and jogged down the driveway with far too much energy for this early in the morning.

As she climbed into the vehicle, she looked at him with wide-eyed concern. "What is it? Is there something on my face? I know, same clothes as yesterday, but my aunt is tiny and doesn't have anything that fits me."

He pulled his gaze from her with a light shake of the head, consciously aware of how his heart had begun to beat a little faster in her presence, and how the suddenly pervasive scent of cinnamon and honey on yesterday's outfit made him want to lean in a little closer.

They were childhood friends reunited by circumstance. That was all. That was all it could ever be, especially with him straight out of Quantico and about to embark on a brand-new career that could take him who knew where.

"Thanks for playing early morning chauffeur," she murmured.

"You're welcome," he said. He yawned, unable to stifle it any longer. "You'll have to direct me to the bakery."

"Back to the main drag and head south."

They drove in silence for a few minutes as Noel racked his brain for the right thing to say. He didn't want to push for details about Daniel's death and risk her closing herself off to him, but on the other hand, he couldn't help unless he had all the information.

"Mina—"

"Take a left here," she said, pointing at the intersection lights ahead of them. Noel nodded and took advantage of the green light to move into the intersection, waiting for a chance to turn. "I did some thinking last night, Noel. I'm worried that—"

He shifted his gaze ever so slightly toward her, ready to listen, when his eyes alighted on something outside the passenger side window.

"No!" He shouted and reached for her as a massive black shape barreled toward them. With a deafening crash, the side of the car crumpled inward, the window shattering as Noel's world descended into darkness.

FOUR

Noel blinked, trying to fight back the black spots that swam in his vision. Why did everything hurt? And why couldn't he move his arm? He blinked again, the dashboard of the vehicle coming into focus. What was he doing inside a vehicle?

The sound of sirens brought everything rushing back. Adrenaline flooded his system, waking him up and sending a rush of strength into limbs filled with shooting pains.

Yasmine. She'd been in the car with him.

"Yasmine? Mina?" He took one look at her and fear gripped his heart. Her head lolled sideways and blood slid down the side of her face. "No, no, no." Emotion suppressed all reason and he unbuckled himself, shoving away the deflating airbag to reach across the center console and press his fingers to her throat.

The pulse of her vein against his fingers

brought a wave of relief tinged with worry. She'd needed to tell him something. She'd been worried and about to confide in him. He clenched his jaw in anger and frustration, wanting to beat his fists on the steering wheel but knowing that giving in to those emotions wouldn't help either of them right now. They needed an ambulance and fast. Just because Yasmine's pulse remained steady didn't mean she wasn't badly injured otherwise.

The sirens grew closer. What was he supposed to do now? Get out of the vehicle? Stay in here until the ambulance arrived? Although the Academy had trained him, finding himself in a life-and-death situation in the real world was new. He hadn't expected to be thrown into a mess like this so quickly, and certainly not on his own before even reaching his first assignment.

Did three attempts on Yasmine's life bring the situation under federal jurisdiction? Probably not. The local PD might want to bring in detectives from the city, keep it in-house and not have to bother with the hassle of turning the whole thing into a federal investigation. Not that Noel could even make that call in the first place. He needed to speak to his FBI mentor at the Buffalo field office. All graduates of the Academy were assigned mentors for their first two years on the job, senior officials whom the new agents could call on for help and advice as needed. Recruits often didn't even get to meet their mentors until their first day on the job, and Noel's case was no exception. Here he was, not even at the office for day one yet, and he already needed his mentor's help.

The paramedics loaded her onto a gurney and strapped her in. He wanted to climb inside the ambulance and go with her, but leaving the scene of the crash wasn't an option, especially not with his credentials and knowledge of crime scene protocol.

"Sir?" One of the paramedics waved at him. "Sir? We need to take her, but I think she's asking for you."

Noel reached her side in seconds. Yasmine's eyelids fluttered, and her mouth moved, forming words he couldn't hear. He bent low, and the curve of her lips sent him tumbling back into a memory he had no place holding in his mind at a time like this. He took her hand, rubbing his thumb across her smooth, golden skin.

"I'm right here, Mina."

She coughed as she tried to speak, sending the paramedics into a frenzy.

"We've got to get her to the hospital," one of them said. "She may be seriously injured."

"Noel?" Yasmine coughed again, and they began to wheel her away. "Noel?"

He grabbed the side of the gurney and stumbled along next to her. "I'm here. I'm listening."

"Need to tell you," she said, whispering so softly that he almost didn't catch what she said.

"Tell me what?" He gripped her hand tighter, struck with a strange fear of what she might say, though he couldn't explain exactly why. "Yasmine, they're taking you to the hospital to get checked over. I'll join you as soon as I can. I'll call your aunt and tell her what happened. Don't worry. It can wait."

"No!" She pulled her hand from his and pressed her fingers against his chest as he leaned over the gurney. "Daniel. We need to talk... Daniel. The person...who killed him. What if...they think..."

A paramedic came around to where Noel stood and pushed in front of him, a scowl on his face. "I'm sorry, sir, but we need to get her out of here."

Noel wanted to jump into the ambulance, to ask her what she meant, to make sure she'd be all right—three attempts on her life in less than twelve hours, how was that even possible?—but the second the paramedics pulled her gurney from his grasp, Officer Wayne appeared and drew him aside.

"You need to have officers follow the ambulance," Noel said to Wayne. "This is the third time someone has tried to kill that woman in twenty-four hours."

Officer Wayne shook his head, and Noel felt an inkling of the frustration with him that Yasmine had shown. "I'm sorry, but I don't have the manpower. Captain's orders. We're short on on-duty officers at this time of the morning."

"What about the guys who came to spell me outside her aunt's place?"

"Already off duty. Look, she'll be fine in the ambulance."

"You don't know that. If you don't send a car to follow in the next five seconds, I'm going to drive off in one of your cars myself." He looked around the intersection again and realized with alarm that something was missing. The vehicle that had hit them. Dread and fury mixed in his stomach. *That settles it. This was a deliberate act.*

Officer Wayne looked Noel up and down with a grimace. "You do look like you need to get to the hospital and get checked over. You were inside the car at the time of the crash?"

"Yes." Noel looked pointedly at the officer he'd thought he'd gotten along with the day before. "We need to go."

Wayne glanced back at the other policemen setting barriers around the crash and directing traffic. "Technically, you should get checked out, too. We can deal with reconstruction later. If Miss Browder dies, we're going to need to do a lot more than just take a few photos. I hate to admit that I was in the wrong, but it sure looks like someone wants Miss Browder out of the way. Guess she was right to be concerned, but I tell you, it's a stretch to think it has anything to do with her brother, and the captain agrees with me."

"She's not going to die." Noel pointed at the police cars in the intersection. Officer Wayne needed to stop talking and have a cop drive him to the hospital. He ground his teeth and touched his coat pocket, where his newly presented badge reminded him of what he'd devoted his life to. "She can't."

Not when I've just found her again.

Noel slipped in and out of consciousness as he reclined in the hospital chair by Yasmine's bedside. The clock above the door read quarter to nine in the morning. He'd hoped to catch up on sleep as he waited for updates, but with nurses constantly coming and going and his mind racing to make sense of events, rest was a long way off.

Yasmine's aunt had already visited and authorized him as a family visitor, and Noel had promised to call her as soon as the doctors or nurses bothered to tell him how Yasmine was doing. She looked pale and attached to too many tubes. His only consolation was that the hospital café opened at nine. He planned to imbibe at least two espresso shots and a large black tea so he could be functional as soon as Yasmine woke.

He stood, stretched, then crossed the room and opened the door, checking to make sure the officers stationed at either end of the hallway were still there. He'd send them on their way once the risk of falling asleep at Yasmine's bedside had passed, but he was deeply grateful to Officer Wayne for convincing the captain to station two patrol guys here this morning. Both Wayne and the captain had agreed that three successive attempts on Yasmine's life were no coincidence. They'd expressed a need to talk to her as soon as she awoke, but Noel wanted to talk to her first.

She had information about her brother's

death that obviously hadn't been taken seriously, that hadn't been included in the official reports. Daniel Browder had been killed in a workplace accident, Officer Wayne had said yesterday, showing him a file full of reports from various investigative parties. Daniel had worked at Newtech Inspections, a facility that manufactured and tested military equipment under contract with the Department of Defense. The entire facility underwent a workplace safety inspection after Daniel's death and the incident had been ruled a tragic accident. Newtech Inspections hadn't been deemed at fault.

Noel sighed and sat back down in the hospital chair. He couldn't imagine what Yasmine must be going through, but all the evidence— the reports, the workplace inspection— pointed to a horrific freak accident. Nothing malicious there. These people after Yasmine, well…either she'd been holding something back and she knew exactly why she'd been targeted, or…frankly, Noel had no idea. People didn't go to such great lengths to take another person's life unless they had a lot to lose. A man had killed himself rather than get brought into the police station for questioning.

"Wake up, Yasmine," he muttered. He stood and paced at the end of her hospital bed.

"There's something big happening here, and I'm ready to listen to whatever you wanted to say."

The only response was the steady, soft beep of the machine beside her. Moments later, a nurse bustled in and greeted him with the tight smile of a person at the end of a long overnight shift. Noel waited until she'd roused Yasmine to check her vitals before asking the question that burned on his tongue.

"How's she doing?"

The nurse adjusted the top of Yasmine's blanket and gave Noel another smile that was far more genuine. "She'll be fine. Bruised and battered and a little worse for wear, but I imagine the doctor will want to discharge her within a few hours. She'll have to take it easy with those fractured ribs, though."

Noel ran his hand down his face. Fractured ribs. That'd be fine to deal with, so long as she didn't have to do any more running from bullets. "No concussion? Internal bleeding? The doctor mentioned checking for those."

"No, we'd know by now if either of those things was an immediate issue. The doctor will want to give her some specific instructions on care and pain management before she leaves, though. With an impact like that, she's very fortunate that her injuries aren't worse.

Somebody was definitely looking out for her."
The nurse flicked her eyes to the ceiling as
she passed Noel.

And it should have been me.

"Noel?" Yasmine blinked slowly, her eyelids heavy with sleep. "You're here?"

He dragged the chair closer to her bedside
and perched on the edge, resting clasped
hands on the side of the bed. "Of course I'm
here. I wasn't going to leave you all alone."

"Call my aunt?"

"She came, but I sent her home. She'll come
again in a bit when I give her an update."

Yasmine sighed, a deep exhalation that
seemed to encompass all of yesterday's strug-
gles. "You don't need to be the one to stick
around, though. Could call one of my friends,
or—" Her eyes opened wide and she tried
to sit up, grimacing at the movement. "The
bakery!"

Noel popped out of his seat and pressed
her shoulders back down. She didn't resist,
but her eyes were desperate with worry. "It's
going to be okay. You need to rest."

"I need to get down there and start baking. There are orders to fill, and Mrs. Deaver
comes in at eleven for tea biscuits for the book
club, and—"

"Can't somebody else handle that? You don't run the place on your own, right?"

Yasmine's eyes filled with tears, and he felt as though he'd been the one sitting in the passenger seat during the crash. He'd seen her cry once before—once and only once—when they were children, after the death of a family pet. This bakery meant a lot more to her than he'd assumed.

"You're telling me you run an entire small business by yourself, with no one to help you?"

She turned her face away from him as though realizing what she showed him by allowing the tears to form. "I've been back here for only eight months. I'm hoping to hire an assistant soon, but I can't afford it yet. This is my business, my life. You have no idea what kind of repercussions it has when a small business closes its doors without warning on a regular business day. People go elsewhere, and it starts a ripple effect."

"It's only one day, Yasmine."

She looked at him then, and though her eyes were red and wet, the ferocity of her expression almost sent him stumbling backward. "I didn't ask you to stay, Noel. If you're going to stand there and question my knowledge about my business, then I'm going to have to ask you to leave."

Ouch. But she made a good point. "Fine. But I'm not exaggerating when I say that you can't go in to work today. I'll call my mother. She's a good baker. I'm sure she can handle the basics. You have recipes?"

"Yes." Yasmine sighed again and closed her eyes. "I can't believe I'm going to say this, but call my aunt, too. She...well, some of the recipes are based on ones I learned from her and my mother."

"Done." He searched his contact list for his mother's number. "They'll need a key, right?" But when his eyes flicked from his phone screen to Yasmine, her face was relaxed and her breathing steady. She'd fallen back asleep.

She needed her rest in order to heal, and Noel wasn't going to be the one to deny her that. He crossed the room with soft steps as the number connected and began ringing. He opened the door and slipped out, pulling it shut behind him. The phone rang for a fourth time when, out of habit, Noel glanced both ways down the hall.

And then did a double take. The policemen who'd been stationed there were gone.

"Hello?" His mother's voice came through

the receiver. "Noel? I didn't hear from you last night. Is everything all right?"

"Sorry, Mom. Something's just come up. Can you call Yasmine's aunt and talk to her about opening the bakery for Yasmine today? Wish I could say more. Gotta go." He hung up and dialed the station.

"Good morning, Newherst Central Police Station. Officer Rygel speaking."

"Hey, Rygel? It's Special Agent Black. You happen to know if the guys stationed down at Newherst General were recalled? They on shift change a few minutes early or something? Thought they weren't scheduled to leave until nine."

"Oh, hey, Black. No, they should be there. Wait, hang on." The sound of yelling came through a muffled receiver. "There was a disturbance on the second floor, a violent patient who grabbed a sharp tool off a tray. He required restraint and use of force. Our guys went to help out. They're not back yet?"

"Nope. Might want to do something about that." He ended the call and slipped the phone in his pocket. *Could be nothing,* he tried to tell himself. *You're on edge from the wreck and everything that happened yesterday. This is a hospital. This kind of disturbance happens all the time.*

A doctor approached from the end of the hall, holding a clipboard and flipping through the attached sheets. He turned toward Yasmine's door.

"Hey. Hey!" Noel shot his arm out and stopped the doctor from turning the handle. "She just fell asleep again. Can't you guys coordinate these things? This constant waking up can't be good for patient health."

The doctor tapped his chart. "Routine procedure, sir. We only have the patient's best interests at heart."

Of course. He trusted the doctors and nurses, sure, but how could she be expected to recover without proper rest? "Fine. You going to be in there long?"

"At least five minutes."

Noel nodded and waited until the doctor entered the room before catching the attention of a nurse working at the central desk of the ward. "Hey, can you make sure no one else enters that room? I'm going to step away for two minutes. If you see anyone approach that shouldn't be there, sound the alarm. I'm not joking."

The nurse nodded at him with frightened eyes. Good. Two minutes was all he needed to run down to the second floor and find those officers and get them stationed back in place if they weren't already on the way. With the doctor in Yasmine's room for five minutes and the staff watching out for her, there wasn't anything to worry about. Two minutes, maximum. That's all.

He ran down the hallway and took the stairs, making it to the second floor in under twenty seconds flat, then continued to that ward's central desk in another three seconds. He slammed his hands on the desk to catch the nurse's attention. "Where was the disturbance? Which room?"

"Sir?"

Noel pulled out his FBI shield and flashed it at the nurse. "There were two officers down here helping out. Did they go back up to four?"

The nurse regarded him in utter bewilderment. "N-no, there were no officers. Everything's been quiet down here all night. You're supposed to be upstairs, aren't you? I just sent Dr. Lawrie up to see you."

"I know. I passed him already. He's doing the check-up right now."

"She."

Noel froze. "Excuse me?"

"She. Dr. Lawrie is a woman."

Noel didn't waste time. He bolted back the way he'd come, pushing aside the fear as he took the steps two at a time. Less than a minute. He'd been gone less than a minute. She'd be all right. Just a misunderstanding. It had to be, because a fourth attempt on her life in less than twenty-four hours would be ludicrous.

He burst through the door of Yasmine's room. The doctor had a syringe poked into Yasmine's IV bag and was pushing a fluid into it.

Noel brought his gun up in a flash. "Drop it and step away from her."

The doctor stared at Noel in surprise, then anger, but didn't release the syringe. "I'm trying to help a patient, sir."

"You can help her by stepping aside." Noel came closer, hoping to deescalate the situation without discharging his weapon inside a hospital.

"I'm afraid I can't do that." The doctor removed the syringe and placed it on the rolling metal medical cart at the end of Yasmine's bed. "You see, she's quite critical."

That didn't make sense. "I thought she was going to be fine."

The doctor shook his head and gripped the cart's handle as though to wheel it from the room. "I'm afraid not. And neither will you, if you continue interfering."

Before Noel could react, the doctor shoved

the heavy cart at him. The distraction gave the doctor the split second he needed to lunge, duck and roll past Noel, then rise to his feet and sprint out the open door.

"Hey!" Noel pushed the cart away, then reached across the bed to yank out the IV tube from the bag before taking off after him. He shouted at the central desk as he flew past, "Call the police and get those officers back here, now!"

One minute. He'd left her for one minute. What was going on?

Yasmine awoke with a gasp. Pain flooded her limbs, and the sounds of beeping, wailing machines and anxious voices sent her head spinning. Or maybe that was the pain's doing. So much noise, so much blurred motion around her, and everything hurt.

When she came to for a second time, the noises and people were gone. Her head throbbed with a dull ache and her vision had cleared. Noel stood at the end of the hospital bed, staring at her with such intensity it was a wonder he didn't set the hospital room on fire.

"Hey," she said, but it came out as a harsh croak. Her throat felt scratchy, dry. Noel must have read her mind, because it took only seconds for him to offer her a glass of water, slipping his hand underneath her head and tilting the glass to her lips. She couldn't remember ever being so grateful for a drink of water before, but it felt marvelous as it slid down her throat and cooled her from the inside.

"Take it easy," Noel said, pulling the glass away. "You've had a rough morning."

He placed her head back down on the pillow but kept his hand on her cheek. Yasmine wasn't sure if she felt grateful for the gesture or if it made her anxious. She could barely recall what had happened after she'd left Auntie Zee's house this morning.

"What happened?"

Noel's eyebrows dipped with worry. "What do you remember?"

"Not much. We left my aunt's place." The words were difficult to form, but getting easier as the grogginess wore away. "Then, it's blurry. We were in the car…"

"There was an accident. We got hit by another vehicle when we entered an intersection."

In alarm, Yasmine tried to wiggle her toes and fingers. She felt them all move and the fear eased. "And I got the worst of it, obviously. You're okay, though?"

He nodded and brushed away a lock of hair that had fallen over her eyes. "You took a direct hit, but thankfully the car I borrowed is new and has airbags and tons of other safety features. I mean, thankfully for us. Not so much for the car's owner. I'm going to let Wayne explain that one to his friend."

"Can I go home soon?" She wanted to crawl into her own bed, snuggle down in the warm sheets and sleep without the smell of lemon and ammonia in her nostrils. Noel didn't react, and her heart sank. "I can't, can I?"

"Afraid not. Your apartment is still a crime scene."

She'd forgotten about that, but with the memory of the apartment shooting came the additional memory of the sniper at the restaurant. An image of the man swallowing something and dying before the police could take him in came too readily to mind, bringing a wave of anxiety and a sudden feeling of helplessness. "Noel…what's going on?"

He sighed and rested his elbows on the side of the bed. "I was hoping you could tell me. We need to take you someplace safe to talk."

"Can't we talk here?"

He looked over his shoulder, and Yasmine followed his gaze to the door. He looked uncertain, almost nervous. "No."

"Why? What aren't you telling me?" The

look on his face made her nerves flare again. "Noel! The bakery!"

"We took care of that already, earlier. Your aunt and my mom have it under control. You really don't remember?" His face remained expressionless as she told him she didn't. "Yasmine, there was an attack a few hours ago inside the hospital. Someone posing as a doctor tried to insert a foreign substance into your IV line. I wasn't able to catch him in time, but the police are still searching for the man based on my description. I got a good look at him. He won't be able to hide for long."

She swallowed hard on the lump in her throat. Her stomach flared with either nerves or nausea caused by whatever had been in the IV—she really couldn't tell which. "Here? How did he get in the hospital? Are you all right?"

"I'm fine, but I should be asking *you* that question." His eyelids drooped as he looked away from her, a raw sadness clear across his face.

She wanted to reach out to him, but she wasn't sure how he'd react. Would he accept comfort from her, or would that still be too familiar after so much time apart? "What is it?"

He shrugged. "I guess… I'm just sorry that

there isn't anyone else here with you. That you're stuck with a childhood friend you barely know instead of...uh, never mind."

Yasmine laughed. "Now you sound like my aunt. Trust me, it's better this way."

"So there's no special someone in your life?"

"I'm unattached. Unencumbered. I have an entire business to get off the ground, and settling down would only get in the way of that. Maybe someday, but the timing is no good."

"There wasn't anyone in Amar?"

Yasmine felt the doors shut inside of her. Yes, there was someone in Amar, a part of the story she'd left out last night when she'd told Noel about leaving Newherst. Yes, she'd loved Marc very much, or at least, she'd thought she did. But when she caught Marc cheating on her with a superior officer, she'd walked away from him without a second thought. He'd been a liar and a cheat, and she had too much self-respect to listen to his excuses or accept his halfhearted apologies. That didn't mean that it hadn't hurt, or that it hadn't left a scar of betrayal across her heart.

When she didn't answer Noel's question, he sighed again and leaned back in his seat. Yasmine couldn't deny that she liked having him here. She was grateful that he'd taken the time to make sure she was all right, and under different circumstances, their reunion might have been pleasant. Welcome, even. His features, so similar to those of his younger self but now matured, brought back the flurry of conflicted emotions she'd tried to shove away last night.

"Thanks for sticking around," she said. Suddenly the memory of their conversation in the car the day before came flooding back. "Even if I didn't."

Noel's tired eyes widened and his shoulders slumped. "That's in the past, Mina. Let's move on. There are greater things at stake here than hashing out old hurts."

"Even if the hurts aren't as old as we try to claim?" She'd seen the anguish on his face. He couldn't hide that, no matter how much he tried to.

Noel shook his head. "We can talk about all this later, okay? As soon as we get the green light to move you from this room, we're heading someplace safe."

"And here I thought the hospital would be the safest place of all."

He pressed his lips together. "I thought so, too, but I was wrong, and I'm so sorry for my error in judgment. You could have been badly hurt or killed, and it would have been my fault."

"Noel, of course not. You can't anticipate everything."

"There's more going on here than either of us understands." He lowered his voice. "I need you to tell me everything you know about Daniel's death and your ten years overseas. Someone is trying very, very hard to kill you, Yasmine. The way things are going, these people are not going to give up until they succeed—unless I stop them first. And that's exactly what I intend to do."

FIVE

A few hours later, Yasmine didn't get the sense that the doctors were planning to discharge her anytime soon. There were several policemen stationed directly outside her door, Noel kept jumping up to talk on the phone with a worried expression on his face and nurses kept coming in to take her blood or ask her how many fingers they were holding up. It was getting tedious.

While Noel was on the phone yet again, a knock at the door revealed a nurse with a tray of lunch. She set up a tray table and raised the bed so that Yasmine could eat while seated. The tray contained a barely appealing meal of meatloaf, mashed potatoes, boiled carrots, yogurt and a banana. A glass of mystery juice sat on the side.

"This is lunch?" she asked the nurse's retreating figure. "I like bananas, at least."

She lifted the glass of juice and sniffed.

It smelled like a combination of orange and grapefruit, and the pale pinkish color suggested that it was probably a citrus-based beverage.

"Don't drink that." Suddenly Noel was beside her, plucking the glass out of her hands. "Do you know that nurse? Did you ask where the food came from?"

Yasmine gaped at him. "First, I wasn't going to drink it because I'm allergic to citrus. Second, she's been in here at least twice today, and third, no, I did not, because why would I?"

Noel grunted and crossed his arms. "We can't be sure it's safe. I want to know that a trusted hospital staff member had eyes on this tray the whole time."

"I mean, I'm sure it's not great food, but aren't you overreacting a little?"

"Did you say you had a citrus allergy? They should know that. Why did they give you this juice?"

Yasmine sighed. As sweet as it was for Noel to be so concerned, he'd leaped to acting overprotective in a single bound. "I wasn't awake to fill out the meal request form, so they just gave me whatever they had the most of. And the allergy thing is probably just an oversight."

"Don't think so." Noel grabbed the tray and slid the contents into the garbage before dumping the juice in the sink. "We'll get you a fresh meal. I'll have someone put eyes on it."

"The police have better things to do than play food manager."

"Then I'll call in backup or do it myself."

"Noel! You're acting absurd!"

Noel stopped pacing and stared at her. His tense features softened. "I'm not. I'm trying to do the best I can to keep you safe, is all. I'm just…I'm still learning, and my hands are tied since right now, all we've got is a local charge of attempted murder. Nothing federal. I have no authority here."

Yasmine understood that. Coming fresh out of training at the Academy and being immediately thrown into a situation with shots fired had to be nerve-racking. "You're doing fine. I'm sure of it. You've been on the phone a lot, so I know you're doing something, at least."

"Oh." His cheeks turned a light shade of rose. "Some of those calls are with my assigned FBI mentor, letting him know what's going on here, but a lot of them are from your aunt or my mom with bakery updates. They keep asking me to tell you stuff, but I figure you don't need that extra stress. They've got it under control."

Yasmine tensed, imagining fires in the kitchen and exploded bags of flour all over her pristine countertops and floors. "It doesn't sound like it, if they keep calling!"

"Trust me. It's fine."

But nothing about his comment seemed fine at all. She pushed the tray table down to the end of the bed and threw off the blankets. Before Noel could stop her, she'd pulled out the IV in her arm and swung her legs over the side. Her brain said that the movements should hurt more than they did—that the dull ache all over and especially around her ribs was being suppressed by some serious pain-killers—but she couldn't stay here a minute longer.

Noel blanched. "What are you doing? You're going to hurt yourself."

"You said the hospital isn't safe. That was hours ago. If someone is out to kill me, they've had time to formulate a new plan, right? I mean, if poisoning my lunch wasn't the new plan."

"Sorry about that. I'll send for more food if that's what you're worried about."

"I'm more concerned about getting out of here and having that talk. Why aren't you?" She stared him down, fully aware that it would be only a matter of time before the painkillers wore off. "I need to find my street clothes."

Noel released a deep sigh as if he'd fought hard to resign himself to her actions. "Stay here. I'll ask them to discharge you and explain why. You're right that it's not safe here. We should get you to the precinct. We can set up a place for you to lie down in one of the rooms there, and I'll make sure you get the necessary pain medication to remain functional. But if I do this and get you out of here, can you promise to take it easy? Listen to the doctor's recommendations?"

"I promise to listen." She smirked at him and he rolled his eyes, like they were children and teasing each other. Only in this case, it was far from a tease. Judging by recent events, it was life or death.

Although it took another hour before they were escorted downstairs to a waiting patrol car, Yasmine was surprised to find herself relieved to be heading back inside the precinct.

After they checked in with Nia at reception, Noel headed down the hall to hold open the door to a small side room with couches, a water cooler and a kettle with teabags and paper cups beside it. "You going to be okay in here? If you feel off at all, you tell me. You remember what the doctor said—it's remarkable that you're alive and escaped the crash with only a few broken ribs and some bruises. Don't try to play the hero. If you think you're going downhill, I'll get you back to the hospital in minutes."

"I'll be fine." Yasmine eased herself down onto a brown-and-orange couch that looked like a castoff from the seventies. The doctor had told her to be gentle on her body, not to move too quickly or do a lot of bending or crouching, anything that might exacerbate the fractures or shift the positions of broken bones. "I'm still not sure how you pulled that off."

"Thank Officer Wayne and Captain Simcoe for that. They need to question you about yesterday's events, anyway."

"Didn't we already do that?" Yasmine shifted a few of the throw pillows so she could lie back and rest her head. "I don't know what else to tell them. I have no idea why people are shooting at me. I didn't ask for this. I didn't see anything at the crash. You saw more than I did. I don't think I asked before, but I take it that we don't know about the other driver?"

Noel shook his head. "I was disoriented for a few seconds from the airbag slamming into my face, and the other car was gone when my vision cleared. A large black SUV plowed right into us. It was deliberate. I already talked to the traffic guys about it. No one barrels through an intersection, makes that kind of hit and disappears without having done it intentionally. The cops put out a BOLO for the vehicle, but nothing has turned up yet. And it probably won't."

Yasmine didn't like the uncertainty in his tone. "Why do you say that?"

He sat across from her and gripped the sides of the chair. "Because yesterday a man killed himself in front of us. He took what was probably a cyanide capsule in a back molar to end his life rather than speak to us. If the crash is connected—and I'm going to say it is—you think whoever's behind it is going to be dumb enough to leave a smashed-up SUV lying around? No way. It'll be fixed by someone behind the scenes or found scrubbed in a parking garage somewhere."

"We don't have parking garages in this town."

"You know what I mean."

Yasmine swallowed down the sudden rush of fear that threatened to sweep her away. She'd been fine managing this so far. She'd felt able to handle it. Noel had mentioned she'd cried about the bakery earlier this morning, but she had zero recollection of that and blamed anything she'd said or done on the pain medication.

"Yasmine?" Noel spoke softly and leaned toward her. With one hand, he closed the door to the room and used his foot to make sure it shut. "We need to talk. For real. About Daniel. And about you."

She didn't want to. She'd put the conversation off time and time again yesterday, and each time she'd felt herself ready to open up, there'd been another attack. He needed to know, though, because if Daniel really was murdered, he might be able to claim jurisdiction or at least get someone up here who could. But it was going to hurt, each and every word.

"Fine," she said. "But can you make me some tea first? This might take a while."

Noel listened closely as Yasmine recounted her conversation with her brother only a few days before his passing. From the sound of things, Daniel had stumbled across information at work that he wasn't supposed to see, but her entire premise was nothing but conjecture. When she explained that Daniel had been found dead shortly after she'd recommended that he talk to his boss about the papers he'd seen, Yasmine paused and looked at Noel expectantly over her paper cup.

"It's a great theory," he said, hoping that she wouldn't hate him for what he planned to say next. "But I'm afraid that's all it is. The reports, the files and the investigation afterward all point to a workplace accident. Not murder. Officer Wayne showed me everything they have on it. I know you're looking for someone to blame—"

Her dark brown eyes widened in disbelief, and he knew immediately that he'd said the wrong thing. "Looking for someone to blame? You think I want to believe my brother was murdered? You think it would make me happy to discover that there's someone out there evil enough to take the life of an innocent man? Right here in my town?"

He didn't think that at all. "So, why are you stuck on this? Do you believe the accident reports were fabricated?"

Yasmine took a sip of tea and lowered the cup, resting it between her hands in her lap. "Noel, I'm not sure you've heard everything. The way you spoke earlier, I thought you knew where Daniel worked and for whom. That you'd read the reports yourself."

She was implying he'd missed something, and that made him feel foolish. "I've read the police report, but like you said, the company manufactures and tests parts for military equipment for the Department of Defense. You think there was something wrong with the numbers for the equipment? You said yourself that you don't even know what Daniel meant by that."

"Think about it. All military equipment is subject to stringent testing measures to ensure it operates the way it's supposed to, so that it won't fail in a critical moment during deployment. What if...what if his boss fudged the inspection numbers?"

It was such a ludicrous suggestion that Noel almost laughed, but he respected Yasmine too much and they'd known each other too long for him to react that way. "I'd say that's incredibly unlikely. Aren't military equipment testing standards handed down by the Department of Defense itself? Surely it'd take notice if equipment started to fail all over the place."

"Yes, but not every piece of equipment will fail. That's the whole point. It happens so rarely that surely it's conceivable testing numbers could be faked for quite some time before anybody caught on. If they ever did."

"You'd have to fool a whole lot of people." Noel considered the logistics of such a scheme. "You'd have to convince some employees to be in on it, too, but you'd be able to move more parts through the line, make more cash. Does Daniel's boss live a lavish lifestyle? Live beyond what his means should be for someone in his line of work? Take many trips?"

Color flushed Yasmine's cheeks, and she raised the cup to her lips as though trying to hide behind it. "I don't know."

That was disappointing. If only she had some clue, some inkling of evidence how this was possible, because right now, the accusation came off like a crazy theory from a person whose imagination worked overtime. And if they eliminated the number-fudging angle, it left one other theory.

Noel braced himself for her anger. "Mina, can you tell me what you were actually doing in Amar?"

She coughed, spitting the tea from her mouth back into the cup. "Excuse me?" Her brown eyes flashed at him. "I lived with my family. Went to the American University of Amar. I graduated *cum laude* with a degree in psychology and an offer to start work at a local practice in Kerat, the capital city."

"That's it?" She was holding something back, he could tell. As recruits, they'd done enough testing on interrogation and reading body language in Quantico that the information was at the forefront of his mind. "I know you're omitting important information, Yasmine. There are people after you, trying to kill you, and we need to know why. I'm just exploring all the angles here."

She looked away, resting her lips on the rim of the cup. "I joined the military."

It was his turn to stare. "You what?"

She raised her chin and looked at him with defiance. "I joined the military, Noel. Learned how to fight, how to shoot, how to defend others."

"But…why?"

"I joined with a friend." She placed her empty cup on the side of the couch. "I had a choice. If I was going to stay in Amar to live and work, to take the position offered at the practice after graduation, I required dual citizenship. Since my mother's family is Amaran and I lived there for years while I was a dependent, the only additional requirement was a year of military service. It's no different than the rule in many countries in the world. Plus, the military there has strong support from the United States. There is a lot of similar training and shared ethics, so I felt comfortable being a part of it."

And yet her behavior still seemed evasive

and closed off when she spoke about her time there. She'd pulled her arms into her sides and hadn't looked at him once during the entire explanation.

"Were you deployed? On active duty?" Maybe she'd made an enemy while in the field.

Yasmine shook her head. "No, never."

"And you're sure there's nothing else?"

Silence stretched from one side of the room to the other as she avoided looking him in the eye. What could she possibly be holding back from him? And why would she do it if it could help them figure out why someone was bent on ending her life?

A knock on the door startled them both. It opened without the person on the other side waiting for an invitation. Nia, the receptionist, poked her head in the room. "Sorry to interrupt, but Special Agent Black? Captain Simcoe has news for you regarding yesterday's incident."

"Thanks, Nia." He rose, enjoying the stretch in his aching legs. All those hours in the hospital chair hadn't done much to help his own bruises heal. "I'll be out in a moment."

Yasmine pushed herself upright, and Noel didn't miss the grimace on her face. The pain medication could do only so much. She'd have to be on top of taking it regularly or she'd be in a world of agony. "I'm coming," she said.

"No, you're not."

She stood before he could make her lie back down, and as much as he wanted to yell at her to make better choices, she was a grown woman and knew her body's limits. At least, he hoped she did. Now that he knew she'd spent a year in the military, however, things about her were becoming a whole lot clearer—like how she'd managed to escape an entire team of black-clad shooters in her apartment, and why she hadn't flinched when he'd drawn his gun in front of her.

"Suit yourself." He held the door open and she exited first. As she passed, he caught another whiff of cinnamon and honey. He'd have to ask his mother to bring something home from the bakery so he could try it. If Yasmine's baked goods tasted as delicious as she smelled, her business would be a hit in no time.

They entered Captain Simcoe's office and sat, Yasmine keeping her back straight so she wouldn't compress her ribs. The captain glanced at Yasmine with concern, then at Noel. "Listen, Black. I'm keeping you in the loop because your uncle down in Pennsylvania was one of the best officers I ever served with, back in my early days. And I know you spent a few years on the force before moving on, so you know how to get along with the fine men and women here at the station. I don't want to see you flounder on your new path, but you have to promise not to interfere. This isn't the FBI's case, but you may be able to get a line on something once you hear what I have to say. Can you keep a lid on it?"

Noel clamped down on his immediate reaction to agree with the captain, recognizing this as the kind of gray area where consulting with his FBI mentor would be the prudent move. Stepping on toes or cutting corners was not the way he wanted to start his career. "As long as there's nothing illegal about me hearing this information or keeping details from my people, I'm on board, but I *will* have to speak with my mentor about it, however vaguely. As soon as I hear anything—"

"You'll pass it up. I know. You're new. Trust me, this is how it works. So, let me break it down for you. Toxicology came back on the shooter with what killed him." The captain slapped a manila folder down on the desk and slid it toward Noel. "Cyanide tooth. Back molar. The kind of stuff you see in spy movies, only it's real. No joke."

Noel pressed the tips of his fingers against

the folder. "So it's officially a suicide. No one got hurt and you could charge him with attempted murder for the shooting, but since he's dead, there's no one to prosecute. Did you find out who he is?"

The captain inhaled slowly and exhaled as he folded his hands together and placed them on the desk. "This is where the situation gets interesting. Open it."

Noel glanced at Yasmine, who shrugged. He flipped open the folder. The top sheet was a profile of the shooter, whom he recognized from the black-and-white photo. "This is definitely the guy."

"Look closer," said Captain Simcoe. "Take in the dates. The occupation."

Noel noticed Yasmine straining to read the sheet from where she sat and adjusted his chair closer to her so she wouldn't have to move and shift her ribcage. He ran his finger down the page and froze on one line. "He was an elite sniper for the US Army." He didn't read the rest of the line out loud. He couldn't.

The sniper who'd taken a shot at Yasmine yesterday, who had swallowed a cyanide pill to escape capture, did not exist.

According to the file in Noel's hands, the man had been killed in action three years ago.

SIX

"That can't be right." Next to him, Yasmine stared at the photo. "There's been a mistake. This can't be the same person."

"But it is," said the captain. "And we still haven't found the vehicle that put you in the hospital. There's something strange going on here, and I don't like it one bit."

Noel slammed his hand on the desk, frustration mounting. As far as he understood it, there was very little he could do right now to help. "Look, I'll be the first to admit that I'm new at this whole Bureau thing, but maybe my mentor will know if there's anything the FBI can do. He's located out of the Buffalo office, where I've been assigned. With a military connection, maybe we can take a terrorism angle on it. The sniper attack and the car crash happened when I was with Miss Browder, so that alone might be enough to give me permission to assist your officers."

"Do it." Simcoe leaned back in his chair, shaking his head. "We'll take any help we can get. This is usually a quiet town, and we've already had to call in extra officers from Buffalo to give us a hand. You may be new to the badge, son, but that also means you can look at evidence and situations with fresh eyes. Maybe draw connections that we jaded uniforms haven't considered."

"Maybe take my reports seriously, for a start," Yasmine muttered.

"I appreciate that, sir. I'll give my mentor a call now. I briefed him about the accident and attacks earlier this morning for the sake of transparency, but maybe he has some suggestions regarding this new information." Noel stood and dialed Special Agent John Crais for the second time that day. He'd spoken briefly with Crais while at the hospital to let him know what was going on and to ask some basic advice, but since the local police were on top of things and the FBI had no cause to get involved, Crais had advised him only to be observant and learn what he could. Now Noel paced back and forth in the small office while the phone rang. Both the captain and Yasmine watched him expectantly, which didn't help the nerves that already roiled inside his stomach. After five rings, his mentor's voice came through the other end.

"Morning, Black. How's the situation?"

"Hey, Crais. Stable but uncertain. We moved the woman out of the hospital about an hour ago, and she's secure at the local police station."

"Got it. Glad she's safe, but Noel, you're there only to support as a friend, right?" The tone of Crais's voice grew gentle but firm. "Whatever the cause of her brother's death, it's not your problem. It's tragic and I'm sorry it happened, but we don't investigate local murders. I repeat this to you because even after leaving the Academy, new agents sometimes have their priorities askew until they get themselves in the rhythm of the Bureau."

"I know, I know." Noel glanced at Yasmine, who still studied the picture of the supposedly dead man who'd attacked them. "But what if I were to tell you that the man who took a sniper shot at Miss Browder was former military?"

"I don't see how—"

"According to government records, he was killed in action three years ago on a mission. His remains were never recovered, but the reports were filed and commendations made. Yesterday, that same man took a shot at Miss

Browder and swallowed a cyanide pill to evade capture. Toxicology confirmed cause of death."

Crais grunted, and Noel waited through a long pause before his mentor spoke. "That does change things. But not for us. That's the kind of bizarre situation that falls under military investigation."

Noel bit down on his tongue, careful to choose his words before speaking. The last thing he needed was for his mentor to think he wanted to operate outside the law, especially on his second day with a badge in his pocket. But if there was anything he could do to keep his childhood friend safe, to give her some answers and some peace of mind about these attacks, he would do it.

"Suppose it gets reported to the military and they decide to investigate," he said, speaking slowly. "How soon would that get underway?"

Crais's response was a clear hedge of the question. "Hard to say. Two, three days? It depends."

"On what?"

"Do you have any evidence linking the sniper to the other attacks? Anything to connect them? Otherwise it looks like an isolated incident."

"You've got to be joking." Noel heard his tone rising, and he tried to rein it back in. "The car accident, hospital attack and even the attack on her apartment can't be considered unrelated to the sniper. Not when they all happened within such a brief window of time."

"We're dealing with a situation outside our control here. The military will likely claim responsibility for investigating only the attack that directly concerns one of their own. You don't have the vehicle that hit you, and you mentioned earlier this morning that the hospital security cameras were too low-grade to use facial recognition software. Does the police department there have a sketch artist? Did anyone get a good look at that guy? If the local police can draw another connection to the military, all involved parties will have to take a hard look at everything that's happened. And if the military takes over, you're not getting answers anytime soon. They have a hard line on information sharing during active cases."

Noel swallowed his disappointment and charged forward. "I saw him, sir. There's an artist coming in from Buffalo, and I'll speak to him when he gets here. But there's one other question."

"Fire away. This is what I'm here for. Though I certainly didn't expect you to be mired in bullets before you even set foot in the office for your first day."

Me either, Noel thought. Yasmine had turned her attention from the photo back to him. Captain Simcoe waited patiently, sifting through paperwork on his desk. Noel was grateful for police help, but resources in this small town were limited. If someone was coming after Yasmine specifically, the persistence of her attackers so far certainly didn't indicate a willingness to give up and leave a job undone. Her life remained in danger, and the longer no one did anything about it, the more difficult it would be to keep her safe. He had one final angle to play with his mentor, and though it was a long shot, he had to try.

He turned his back to Yasmine and lowered his voice. "When I explained the situation surrounding Daniel Browder's death to you earlier, I think I neglected to emphasize a few things. The facility where he worked—their contract was to test pieces of military equipment."

"Yes, you mentioned that." Crais's tone had turned a little terse, and Noel didn't blame him. John Crais likely had better things to do with his time than deal with a paranoid new agent, but Noel plunged on regardless. Backing down from an angle he felt strongly about was not a good quality in an FBI agent, either, so even if Crais disagreed with his assertions, he would still listen and offer advice.

"The testing requirements are handed down by the Department of Defense, and the reports are turned in to someone at the Department directly. I don't know who receives them as I haven't taken this any further, but it occurred to me—what if there's something to Miss Browder's suspicions surrounding her brother's death? What if there really was something going on there? We have a soldier killed in action who reappeared alive and well only to kill himself, plus these other attacks. What if there's a connection between Miss Browder and her brother's work at the facility, some kind of reporting crime between the facility and the Department of Defense?"

Crais grew silent again for several moments. "That's a long shot, Black. But that would definitely provide us with cause to investigate. We could probably make the case that it falls under federal crime, but we're going to need more than that. We can't get a warrant to investigate the place or seize any records without probable cause. And all you've given me so far is conjecture. Good conjecture, so I'm not denying it's a possibility, but this is as far as we can go with what we've got."

Noel pinched the bridge of his nose. He should have taken the ibuprofen they'd offered him at the hospital. He had his own bruises from the car accident, but adrenaline after the attack in the hospital had kept him going until now. The possibility that he might not be able to help Yasmine at all, however, was sucking the energy right out of him.

"Can I go talk to the facility manager? Do I have the right to do that, or are my hands fully tied? A woman's life is on the line. I can't sit by and wait for a bullet to find its mark. Isn't there anything I can do?"

"I'll go."

Noel spun around to see Yasmine standing up, her hand on the back of her chair and her expression resolute.

"Tell him I'm going to the facility," she said. "I need to know the truth about Daniel's death, and I want to hear it from the manager himself."

"No," Noel said, horror rising in his stomach and bringing a wave of nausea at the thought of Yasmine returning to the scene of Daniel's death. Despite her outward show of strength, she couldn't hide the pain behind her eyes, brought on by her own suggestion. "That's a bad idea."

"I'm the only one who can walk in there and get some answers, and I'll go whether you choose to come with me or not."

Her free hand rested on her hip, and Noel felt the blood drain from his face as her sincerity sank in. She would go no matter what he said to talk her out of it—but truthfully, he didn't *want* to. She deserved answers, and her announcement could be the break he needed to get Crais on board with his involvement.

"Did you catch that, sir?"

Crais's sigh from the other end told Noel that Crais had indeed heard Yasmine's declaration of intent. "She can't be dissuaded?"

"I don't believe so, sir. She does have a foreign military background, so she won't be walking in helpless. But she *is* injured from the accident. Broken ribs are the worst of it."

"Well, Black, you're not due to report for work until next Monday. I can't authorize you to visit the facility as a representative of the FBI, but I can't stop you from accompanying her on your own time to keep an eye on her. You're certain she'll go whether you're with her or not?"

Noel shot another glance at Yasmine, who watched him with one raised eyebrow. Yes, she'd do whatever she wanted. She'd proven that the day before when she'd been the one to race out the door in pursuit of the sniper, despite Noel's warnings. And her instincts had turned out to be right.

"She's definitely going to go, sir."

"Fine. Be careful, Black. You're new, inexperienced. If you go on your own accord as backup to look out for her, you'll need to make good use of your training. Read the situation and the people at every step. Stay alert. Don't get caught off guard."

The vise clamped around Noel's stomach eased just a touch. "Thank you, sir."

"Don't thank me yet," Crais growled. "I haven't done anything, and like I said, you're not on the clock, so I can't stop you going on your own time. I can only make recommendations, which I'm doing in this case because you're Academy-fresh and you could use experience with questioning and observation in a real-world context, not because I think this has legs. I don't, not yet, but watch your back, Black. Remember that, as a new agent, a misstep is going to cost a lot more than it would cost someone like me who's been around awhile."

Noel hung up and tapped the phone against his hand. It wasn't the permission he wanted to open a case or the solution he'd hoped for to keep Yasmine safe, but at least he had authorization to go with her while she asked questions. Crais hadn't specifically said whether Noel could flash his badge or not if necessary—just that he was to be careful about it—which seemed like a test. Either way, he'd get in the door, and they could at least explore the possibility of Yasmine's suspicions, ideally getting some answers before the military barged in and took over. If he could also find a reason to open a federal investigation, all the better.

"What's the verdict?" Yasmine's usually authoritative voice sounded soft in the small office. "Look at me, Noel. I'm going."

He turned and placed his hands on the back of his chair. Both Yasmine and Captain Simcoe waited for his answer.

"I can't personally investigate. It falls outside federal jurisdiction."

Yasmine rolled her eyes. "We know. And?"

Noel tried to offer a hopeful smile. "I have permission to go with you as your backup. We can't stop you and neither can the police if you really want to go. But that doesn't mean you have to go in alone."

Yasmine nodded as though she'd expected this outcome. "Got it."

She looked away, her fingers drumming on the back of the chair, and Noel's heart constricted. She acted strong, sure—but how much more pain could she endure before she broke?

SEVEN

Yasmine watched out of the back of the unmarked police vehicle as they approached the facility. Noel sat in front with the driver, listening to police radio chatter come through sporadically. She knew this plan made Noel nervous, but Captain Simcoe had seen the value and offered some help. Two additional police cruisers followed close behind them, though both were marked in an attempt to dissuade any potential attackers from taking advantage of Yasmine being out and about again.

Noel twisted in his seat to look at her. "You all right back there?"

She shrugged. "It's not the most comfortable, but I can handle it."

Concern marked his features. "You're taking your pain medication on time, right? Tell me if you need someone to get anything for you. Most people would still be lying in a hospital bed right now, and before you tell me you're not most people and made of stronger stuff, need I remind you that you are still human?"

She pursed her lips and sighed. The deep breathing hurt a little, too, but the doctor had said she needed to make sure to do that as much as possible. Strange how such a natural function as breathing was a thing she needed to be aware of while healing.

They pulled into the parking lot of the facility. A wave of anxiety washed over her as the sign for Newtech Inspections loomed overhead. Noel stepped out of the vehicle first and opened the door for her, offering his hand to help her out. She ignored it, not because she didn't need his help. More because she didn't want to touch his hand again. It made her insides ache in a different way, and she had enough pain in her life right now. Every time he looked at her, her heart tripped over itself. She kept trying to suppress the rush of emotion that came after that trip, the flood of feelings that she'd thought were long buried and forgotten, but she'd cared for him as deeply as one teenager could care for another all those years ago. And he'd rejected her as fully as any person could, despite the nature of the relationship.

Not that she blamed him for it, not one bit. She'd done the same to him a few years before that. Plus, a lot had changed in ten years, so she wasn't under any illusion that Noel's feelings were resurrecting the same way hers kept attempting to.

Besides, finding Noel attractive was one thing. Admitting to herself that she wished they had another chance was something else entirely, and not something she could afford to do. The loss of Daniel was too recent and the memory of Marc's cheating too clear in her heart and mind. She'd come back to Newherst to escape the heartbreak of Marc's actions, and eight months was not a long time. She had a business to build up, a life to reestablish here.

There was no room for love. None whatsoever.

So why couldn't she help the twist in her stomach as he reached out his hand to her?

"I won't make you do this," he said softly. "I want to learn the truth about Daniel as much as you do. I'm hoping it was only an accident that can be put behind us so you can move on, but I also want to figure out who's after you before anything worse happens."

Yasmine almost laughed at that. "It'd be

hard to get much worse than what's happened so far."

Noel's expression darkened. "It's possible. Trust me."

The intensity on his face took her breath away, and for a moment—just a moment—she thought she saw something else behind his eyes. Something that matched her own emotions. It disappeared just as quickly as she realized that, despite her best efforts, her hand had ended up in his anyway. She pulled it away.

"I'll be right next to you the whole time," he said, his voice low. "If at any moment you need to get out of there or take a break, you let me know. Remember that we have five officers here with us right now, all vetted by the captain. You are safe. I will make sure of it."

Including Officer Wayne, who'd started acting nice to her now that the captain took her seriously. She still didn't care for the man, but she trusted him and the other police officers to do their jobs. She nodded for Noel's benefit and kept her gaze forward, placing one foot in front of the other as they walked toward the main office. She willed her knees not to give way and her lungs not to fail her, and sent up a silent prayer for strength.

Noel pulled open the door to the main of-

fice, and Wayne entered ahead of them. Noel
followed, with Yasmine behind.

"You're up," he murmured.

A small desk and a short padded rolling
chair served as the reception counter in the
center of the main office, but no one sat behind the desk. Yasmine slammed her hand
on top of the little metal bell on the desk's
front corner, and its ding resounded inside
the shadowy space.

"This is the office of a Department of Defense contractor?" Officer Wayne looked behind the desk and took a few steps down a
short hallway that led to several closed office
doors. "Looks pretty sparse. And in need of
serious upgrading."

"You'd think a place funded by government
contracts could afford a nicer working space,"
Noel murmured. "We should check out the
garage and the machinery. Must be folks out
there working."

As they turned to leave, the sound of a door
latch opening halted their progress.

Noel took the few steps he needed to reach
the hallway. "Excuse me, sir?"

The man exiting the room stopped, frozen
in place. "What is it? Who are you?"

"Can we have a word with you, sir?"

"What about?"

Yasmine heard the hesitation in the man's voice. If Noel managed to convince him to come down the hall and he saw the room full of burly police officers, they'd get absolutely no information out of him. She pushed past Noel and stepped into the hallway, ignoring the grunts of frustration from the men behind her.

"Excuse me. My name is Yasmine Browder. My brother is—was—Daniel Browder."

"Browder?" The man's face scrunched up for a moment before recognition dawned. "Oh. Yes. I'm sorry about your brother, miss. Terrible accident."

She took another step forward, swallowing down a sudden wave of grief. "I agree, it was terrible. Would you mind speaking to me for a few minutes about it?"

"About his death?" The man's eyes widened in surprise and then narrowed. "All the right reports got filed. No loose ends. Followed all the procedures."

Loose ends. As if Daniel's death was as mundane an event as a broken glass or an unsent email. If she hadn't thought something fishy was going on at the facility before, based on the look the man was giving her and the way he scrutinized her up and down, she'd have thought so now. "I know, I know. But you have to understand that I've had a very difficult few weeks. Can we speak for a moment? Please?"

The man hesitated and glanced down at his hand still gripping the door handle. Yasmine took another step closer. If she got close enough to him, he might feel pressured to speak to her, to let her inside the office rather than deal with the hassle of kicking her out. When he took too long to respond, she drew on the memories of Daniel to finally allow her suppressed emotions to rise to the surface.

Heat built behind her eyes as tears formed and welled on her bottom lids. "Please. It will only take a moment."

The man's concern and suspicion turned to alarm as Yasmine felt one teardrop slide down her cheek. A dirty trick? Not at all. If she didn't talk to this man, Noel might not have enough information to open an investigation, and she'd have to live with the knowledge of Daniel's murder and the lack of proof for the rest of her life. She missed him *so much.*

"Yeah. Yeah, sure. Come in. Can't be long, though. I got a meeting to head to."

"Thank you so much." She looked back at Noel and nodded. He strode down the hallway to meet her. "My friend will be joining me. As I'm sure you understand, I don't like to travel alone during this difficult time."

"Sure, sure." The man didn't even look at Noel as he reopened his door and let them inside. He walked around to the back of the desk and shuffled some papers, sliding a few loose sheets underneath a blue folder.

Yasmine cut her eyes to Noel to see if he'd noticed, but he wasn't letting on that he'd seen anything at all. Were the police officers in the hallway and front office taking the opportunity to look around? She hoped so.

"You were Daniel's boss?" Yasmine said, breaking the awkward silence. She sat down on an uncomfortable metal chair, wincing at the compression of her ribs. "Anthony…?"

"Clarke." Anthony Clarke extended his hand to Yasmine and then Noel. "Manager of this facility. Your brother did fine work here. Hard worker. Always turned in his reports on time. Hasn't been the same without him."

Yasmine didn't miss the absence of emotion in the man's voice when he spoke about Daniel. "He did love his job and often commented how smooth this place ran," she said, hoping to win Anthony's trust with flattery. And for the most part, she spoke the truth. "With his engineering background, he liked knowing that the work he did made a real difference. He believed in the safety of our troops and appreciated the dedication of the other workers here."

"Yeah? Yeah." Anthony tapped the tip of his finger on the desk. A gold wristwatch slid out from underneath the cuff of his shirt and settled at his wrist. "Excellence or nothing. We have big contracts here. Can't afford to turn in sloppy work. Gotta bring the boys back home in one piece."

"This is a large facility," Noel said, craning his neck to look around the office as though he saw the entire building from where he sat. "I imagine that as a facility contracted by the Department of Defense, you must move a lot of parts through here. You must have a very streamlined testing procedure. Also, that's a very nice watch."

"Huh? Yeah. Gift from my wife." Anthony pushed the wristwatch back under his rolled shirt cuff. "We get large orders. Gotta move it through. Quota or bust. But always excellence."

Noel reached across the desk and picked up a photo of Anthony posing in front of an old convertible. Yasmine didn't recognize the year—as much as she appreciated old cars, she wasn't familiar with all the details like Daniel had been—but she knew that it was definitely expensive and, combined with the expensive gold watch on the man's wrist, definitely outside his pay grade.

"That's a nice car," Noel said. He whistled, shaking his head. "Let me guess. You restore old cars? You must be into that kind of thing, working with machinery and such."

Anthony laughed. "Naw, man. Got it at an auction. Best purchase I ever made."

"Recent?" Noel looked at Yasmine and held up the photo so she could get a better look.

"Yeah, last year. Next auction's coming up in a month in Jersey. Got my eye on another baby. 1991 GMC Syclone. Wanted one of those trucks for as long as I can remember, and better believe I'll be paying whatever it takes to get my hands on her. You know Jay Leno's got one?"

"Those are pricey. Only a few thousand Syclones were ever made." Noel put the photo back on the desk. "I wouldn't have thought a guy on your salary could afford that kind of thing."

Anthony smirked and leaned back in his chair. "All about the savings, man. You got to find ways to cut corners in your life to afford nice things, know what I'm saying?"

"Does that apply to your workplace as well?"

"Hey!" Anthony sat upright, face reddening. "What are you implying?" He looked at Yasmine. "I thought we were here to talk about your brother."

Yasmine took a deep breath and plunged forward. "We are, Mr. Clarke. Shortly before his death, my brother came into this office to speak with you about something. He'd noticed a discrepancy on some reports on your desk pertaining to numbers he'd handed in. He wanted to bring it to your attention to make you aware of any potential problems that you might not have noticed, especially since the inspections are handled through a Department of Defense contract. He knew that if you handed in inspection reports containing discrepancies, even accidentally, and they got flagged, the facility could lose its contract."

As she spoke, she watched the man across from her grow increasingly uncomfortable. He folded his hands on the desk, then dropped his hands to his lap, shifted in his seat, looked around the room and anywhere else but at her. When the manager stared at the desk instead of looking her in the eye, she had a terrible sinking feeling.

Anthony Clarke knew exactly what was going on at his facility, and she felt more certain than ever that what Daniel said to him had gotten him killed.

"Do you remember that conversation, Mr. Clarke?" She glanced at Noel before looking back to the manager. Noel watched him carefully, and she noticed that his hand had crept inside his jacket toward his concealed weapon.

A moment of heavy silence fell over the office before Anthony spoke again. "Yes. I remember. Daniel spoke to me about this, bringing ridiculous accusations." Yasmine's ears perked up. She'd said nothing that specific, and neither had Daniel. "I told him he spoke crazy and if I heard that kind of talk bandied about on the shop floor, he'd be right out the door faster than he could walk."

"Are you admitting that you threatened Mr. Browder?" Noel's arm tensed. Yasmine held her breath.

Anthony turned his attention to Noel as if he'd only just noticed him in the room despite having spoken to him several times... as though he'd written Noel off until this moment. "Excuse me? And who do you think you are?"

Yasmine's heart sank. Noel couldn't lie once he'd been asked directly. Until now, he'd been acting as a friend and travel companion. With the manager's question, his role shifted, and if word got back to the wrong people, he could be in a lot of trouble.

Noel reached inside his jacket pocket and pulled out his badge, flipping it open and then sliding it back inside his pocket. "Noel Black, FBI."

Anthony shot to his feet and pointed at the door. "Get out. You got no right to be in here."

"Did you threaten Daniel Browder, Mr. Clarke?"

"I don't have to talk to you." He grabbed a pile of files off the desk and shoved them into a drawer, locked it, crossed his arms. "I want a lawyer."

"You're not being interrogated or arrested. Miss Browder came to ask a few questions about her brother. Now, what's this about falsifying reports?"

The man's face grew bright red. "Who told you that was happening? There's no way you can know about that. You have no proof."

"No, but my brother suspected it, and now we know the truth." Yasmine's head buzzed with adrenaline. Noel had used their suspicions to verbally coerce the man into an admission. "I said he came to talk to you about discrepancies on some papers he saw. Your response just confirmed that those discrepancies were actually false reports."

Noel stood, matching Anthony's stance. "So, you've been making false reports to the Department of Defense. Maybe sliding a few parts through inspection to increase output? How much extra is that putting in your pocket, Mr. Clarke? I'm guessing it's more than pocket change, based on what we've seen here today."

The manager's jaw tensed so tightly that a thick blue vein stood out on his temple. "Get out! I'll call the police! I'll—"

"Everything all right in here?" Officer Wayne poked his head around the corner. "Black?"

"Who are you?" Anthony pointed at the officer. "What are you doing on my property? I'll charge you all with trespassing! I'll report everything to the captain! I'll—"

Noel touched Yasmine on the shoulder, and she stood. "I think we have everything we came for," Noel said. "Thank you for your time, Mr. Clarke. I suspect we'll be seeing each other again soon."

"You've invaded my privacy by coming here," the man shouted behind them. Noel pushed Yasmine in front of him so that she wouldn't have her back to the manager as they exited.

"Move slowly to the door," Noel murmured,

"then have the officers take you back to one of the vehicles. This man is unstable, and I want you out of here."

Yasmine swallowed the rising lump in her throat and did as he said. She'd been right. She knew that now, even if Anthony Clarke hadn't said as much. Daniel's death hadn't been an accident.

So why, instead of feeling validated about her suspicions, did she feel like things were about to get a whole lot worse?

As police officers ushered Yasmine to the car, Noel paid close attention to Anthony Clarke. They'd clearly rattled the man, but instead of acting ashamed, he'd turned angry—borderline enraged—and Noel didn't want Yasmine anywhere close to what could become a volatile situation. Behind him, Noel heard Clarke follow them out of his office, the telltale tinny sound of a cell phone dialer echoing in the dim hallway. If only Noel could hang around and listen in on the conversation, figure out who Clarke was talking to. He'd already pushed the situation too far, however, and the next step involved getting Yasmine out of here and someplace safe.

He found which car she'd been stowed in and slid onto the seat next to her.

"You doing okay?"

She shrugged and stared out the window. "I guess."

"You were right." He reached across and hovered his hand over her knee, uncertain whether he should place it there to offer comfort or if it would make her upset instead. He pulled away, taking the safe route. "I mean, we don't have physical evidence yet, but I'd think that conversation is enough to earn us a warrant."

"On hearsay? He'll deny everything." Her voice had a distant, listless quality to it. It didn't sound like her. He thought she'd be relieved that they were a step closer to the truth—a small step, but any progress helped.

"Look, I need to call my mentor and tell him what we learned. It might be enough to get the FBI involved, to make this an official investigation."

"You really think so?" She finally turned her face toward him, but the hope in her voice wasn't reflected in her expression. "They'll send guys up from somewhere else, won't they? I mean, you're new. I'm not trying to be callous about it, Noel, but—"

"No, you're right." She made a good point. "But that's not entirely a bad thing. If the FBI sends experienced agents to take over, I should be able to observe even if I can't officially help. I don't report to my assigned office until next week." He pulled out his phone and dialed Special Agent John Crais.

"Black? I didn't expect to hear from you so soon."

"Hey, Crais. We went to the facility and talked to Anthony Clarke, the manager. The guy was jumpy, evasive. When Browder asked him about a conversation with her brother, the guy panicked and revealed information that we didn't have—basically admitted to falsifying inspection reports, but we have no solid evidence. I think he's keeping copies of the reports on the premises, however, or at least some papers that could be considered incriminating. He's also got expensive tastes, though his facility doesn't keep up the same image. Think there's enough to get a warrant?"

"That *is* something." Crais paused, and Noel heard the sound of tapping across a keyboard. "Any other relevant details?"

Noel glanced over at Yasmine, who once again regarded him with one eyebrow raised. He slipped his hand over the phone's speaker and whispered to her. "Your face is going to stick like that one of these days."

The mask broke, and a tiny smile crept across the corner of her mouth as she rolled her eyes and stuck her tongue out at him. He hadn't realized how much he'd wanted to see her smile, and how much he'd wanted to be the one to cause it to appear, until that moment.

"Black? Did Clarke say anything else?"

Noel snapped back into focus. "That's about it, sir. He said that Daniel Browder spoke to him about an issue Browder discovered with the inspection numbers and made what Clarke called ridiculous accusations about falsified reports. That's enough, isn't it? We can take it from here? If we can jump on this before the military gets wind of it and tries to fold it under their own investigation—"

"Where are you now, Black?"

Noel's words caught on his tongue. What did that have to do with anything? "I'm traveling back to the local precinct. Then we'll move Browder to a safe place where she can rest and recover. Is there an FBI safe house in the area?"

"Sounds like we have a lot to talk about. Can you get away from the local police for a little while?"

"Sure, but I don't know what good that's going to do. They've been nothing but cooperative on this, even without it being officially our investigation." Crais's silence through the phone felt heavy and patronizing, and Noel felt his confidence falter. *Stop it*, he told himself. *You're not expected to know everything after only twenty weeks of training. That's what having a mentor is for.* "What's the next step, sir?"

"There's a safe house on the outskirts of Buffalo. You know how to find it. Meet me there in two hours."

As much as Noel didn't want to admit it, the thought of meeting Crais face-to-face brought considerable relief. Crais would know what to do. He'd know how to keep Yasmine safe while playing inside the lines of FBI jurisdiction. Noel didn't have enough experience to do that yet, let alone skirt it in the way he'd done by going inside the Newtech Inspections building.

"Done. See you there."

"Black?"

"Yeah?"

"Don't tell anyone. From what you've said so far, you don't know who you can or can't trust. Somebody knew how to find that woman you're with, so think about who you've been spending time with these past twenty-four hours. Who has had access to your location? Who has known exactly where you were since this began? Who's been pulling strings to get eyes on this woman?"

Noel's breath caught as Crais ended the call. The man made an excellent point. Noel flicked his gaze to Officer Wayne in the driver's seat and then to Yasmine.

"What?" She leaned her head against the window.

"Don't do that." He tugged on her shoulder. "Sit up. That's not good for your injuries, and it makes you a bigger target."

"The windows are tinted, Noel. It's fine. And I'm fine." He shook his head, and she stared at him like he'd grown a second head. "What is it?"

He tipped his chin toward Officer Wayne and then back to the cars behind them. He kept his voice low and quiet, hoping he wouldn't be heard over the crackling noise of the police radio on the dash.

"We might have been going about this the wrong way. Think about it. Who knew your whereabouts this whole time? Since that first incident at your apartment?"

She shook her head. "You're being obtuse. I have no idea."

He hoped that Crais was wrong about this. Noel didn't think his instincts were that bad, but then again, he'd been holding a badge for all of a day and a half. And he had to admit a bias for the work of local police, having spent time as a police officer himself elsewhere in the state. But John Crais had been at this for a long time, a very long time, and had become a figurehead at the Buffalo field office as special agent in charge. Noel was very fortunate to have been paired with him as a mentor, and the last thing he wanted to do was disappoint the man before they'd even officially begun working together.

He inclined his head a second time toward Officer Wayne. Him? No. A string-puller, Crais had said.

"The police?" Yasmine mouthed.

Noel nodded and pointed his finger up. *Higher.* "The captain."

EIGHT

Noel watched as Yasmine deflated in front of him. The faster they got this solved, the faster she could move on with her life. Find peace again. He couldn't even imagine what she was going through—she'd had three weeks to come to grips with Daniel's death, and now here she was being emotionally dragged through it all over again.

"We're going to take down the people who did this," he murmured. This time, when he reached for her knee, he didn't hesitate. She didn't flinch, and a part of him relaxed. But just a tiny part. "Your family has been through enough. *You've* been through enough."

She leaned over to whisper in his ear, and for a moment Noel almost forgot why they were in the back of a police car. The scent of her hair, her skin, transported him to an imaginary time when they could sit together, sip tea and talk. Someday. Maybe someday. As friends.

It didn't matter how his stomach tensed and his mouth dried when she looked into his eyes. He had a brand-new career, an assignment for two years at the Buffalo field office, and after that he might be sent anywhere in the country. Settling down couldn't happen anytime soon, which meant his heart couldn't get distracted, either. Not that Yasmine would ever consider actively distracting him. They'd missed that boat long ago.

"Do you have another car?" she asked.

He shook his head and considered their options. "My parents. I'll borrow their car. When we get to the station... Hang on. We'll need to move on the fly with this." Noel sent a quick text to his mother, asking her to come pick them up. He didn't like the idea of bringing his mom down to the police station or want to interrupt her in helping out at the bakery, but he and Yasmine needed to get away from the station for a while to meet Crais, and he needed to work through all of the details so far in his head. He wanted to be inconspicuous about the absence, just in case there was something to Crais's suspicions.

One thing nagged at the back of his mind as his mom texted back to let him know she was on her way. If the captain was after Yasmine, why had he let her rest at the station? Why not just shoot her or take out both of them some other way?

Because you're a federal agent. And because you've been next to Yasmine since this all began, and he was waiting to find out what you know.

It explained the disappearance of the policemen in the hospital and how the man posing as a doctor had known which room she was in. It also explained the break-in to Yasmine's apartment and the early-morning car accident—she had a regular routine, making her an easy target for stalking and attack. She was even inside a vehicle loaned to Noel by none other than Officer Wayne, someone who'd certainly communicate that information to the captain if asked. On the other hand, it didn't explain the deceased soldier reappearing, alive and well, to take a shot at Yasmine through the restaurant window. Nor did it explain *why* any of this had happened.

He needed to speak to Crais in person. His mentor would know what to do, or at least help clarify the next step to take.

Eventually the convoy of police cars arrived back at the station, with Officer Wayne thoughtfully pulling up to the front door for

Yasmine's sake. Noel scanned the parking lot until he saw it—his mother's bulky white Lincoln.

"Ready? Head straight for the white tub on the left. Don't stop. Get inside and get down."

Yasmine nodded, her expression uncertain. "What are you going to do?"

"Buy us some time. Go now." They exited their respective sides of the vehicle, and Yasmine moved as quickly as her injuries allowed toward his mom's car.

"Hey!" Officer Wayne called and waved his arms. He turned to Noel, concern etched across his features. "Where's she going? Isn't she supposed to stay with us?"

"New plan," Noel said. "I have direct orders from the FBI to take her to a safe house. Tell the captain I'll speak with him soon."

Officer Wayne frowned. "Can't you go in and tell him yourself? We took a whole convoy to protect her, so if you just take off—"

"Trust me." Noel laughed, not even needing to force it. "Nobody's going to suspect a thing while she's in that massive boat, so long as we get moving. Urgent change of plans. Tell the captain to call the FBI if he has questions."

Officer Wayne nodded, still uncertain. Noel knew he'd get a call from the captain in a matter of minutes, so he needed to make the most of whatever brief respite he could grab from all the voices and imminent threats.

He jogged to his mom's car and climbed into the passenger seat. Yasmine lay across the backseat, her teeth clenched as she maneuvered to find a comfortable position with her injuries. Noel fastened his seat belt as his mother pulled out of the parking lot, her lips pursed with disapproval.

"She should be in the hospital," she finally said.

"Yes, Mom. Thanks. But it's not safe there. I need you to pay very close attention to the road while I watch around us. You're going to drive back to the bakery, and then we're going to borrow your car. Okay?"

She clucked her tongue and shook her head. "Noel, I don't like this."

"I promise I'll pay for repairs if it gets scratched."

"I don't care about that! Who'll repair you or poor little Yasmine? She looks more than scratched, and if anything happens to either of you—"

"It won't." Noel hoped he sounded more confident than he felt. "It won't, all right?"

"I hope you're praying for safety and asking God for guidance. I'm praying every chance I get, and more."

And it's not making much of a difference, is it? "Thanks, Mom. But this situation is beyond prayer."

His mom glared at Noel as they reached a red light. "Beyond prayer? Did I hear those words out of my son's mouth?"

"Mom, I—"

From the backseat, Yasmine's quiet voice chimed in. "You did. I heard them, too."

The light turned green, and his mother accelerated. He could almost feel the disappointment through her acceleration. "My own son. I thought I raised you right. You know God cares, no matter what. Nothing is beyond His care. Nothing."

A heavy silence descended inside the vehicle. Noel didn't want to argue with his mother, and he needed to focus his attention on watching everything around them. The tension in his shoulders had only grown from hour to hour, ever since he'd confronted the false doctor in Yasmine's hospital room. He felt as though he was counting down the minutes waiting for the next attack, blind to where it would come from and helpless to stop it.

If it came at all, it would be too soon.

When they reached the bakery, Yasmine had to dig her fingers into the car seat to stop herself from running inside the store. She wanted to sit up and see how busy the parking lot was today, to go inside and take charge and make sure everything was being done right. Noel's mother slid out of the car with a few semi-encouraging words—mostly a vague assurance that she and Auntie Zee had things under control, which didn't do a lot to soothe Yasmine's nerves—and Noel climbed into the driver's seat.

"Wait there one minute," his mom called over her shoulder.

"She gets thirty seconds," Noel muttered. "We need to go."

Less than a minute later, Mrs. Black poked her head back into the car and plopped a paper bag down on the now-empty passenger seat. "A few rolls and some cookies. Zara and I thought you might need them after the day you've had." She pulled two bottles of water out of her purse and handed them to Noel.

"Thanks, Mom."

"You're welcome. Be safe, Noel." She rounded the car to lean in and kiss her son's cheek, sending a pang through Yasmine's insides. She didn't often think of her parents—tried not to, in fact—but seeing how tenderly Mrs. Black treated her son made Yasmine regret that she hadn't appreciated her own mother's affections more when she'd had the chance.

"Thank you, Mrs. Black."

Noel's mom waved at her. "You'll keep praying for him, won't you?"

Yasmine grinned. "Of course I will."

"God loves you, honey." She disappeared from sight as Noel pulled the car away, a slight scowl on his face.

"You don't need to pray for me," he muttered. "I can take care of myself. It's you I'm worried about."

"I'll be fine, as long as I get one of those rolls."

At the next stoplight, Noel parceled out the goodies. Yasmine's mouth watered even before her first bite, and although she'd been nervous about Mrs. Black and Auntie Zee running the bakery today and getting the recipes right, one bite into the first roll and she knew she'd worried for nothing. They had it under control.

Noel, on the other hand, did not. Every time he glanced in the rearview mirror, she caught a glimpse of the intensity on his face. His big brother efforts to keep her safe were appreciated, but she had military training. She knew how to take care of herself. If it weren't for a few cracked ribs, it'd be business as usual.

Technically it still could be, so long as she didn't attempt any heavy lifting or bending—cracked ribs were nothing compared to what could have broken.

For Noel's sake, she hoped that this mentor of his could shed some light on their situation. If Captain Simcoe was involved, why? Financial kickbacks? It made sense in a strange and twisted way, but she had a hard time believing that the competent and cooperative captain had a bad bone in his body. She'd met him before, after Daniel's death, and found him both friendly and empathetic, despite his unwillingness to pursue her suspicions. But what did she know, really? Military training wasn't the same as FBI training, and the FBI wasn't the same as—

Her train of thought sparked an idea.

"Hey, Noel? Do you have a way to access financial records or anything like that? Maybe take a look at the facility's emails?"

Noel shook his head. "We'd need a warrant or subpoena for those kinds of records, and the FBI would have to take over the investigation first. I'm hoping to convince Crais to do that when we meet up. I don't have the authority for it, not yet."

They lapsed back into silence as they drove. She didn't want to distract Noel from paying close attention to the road, and truth be told, she didn't know what else to say. Her eyelids drooped as the hum of the car's engine tugged on her muscles and forced her to relax.

"We're here." Noel's hand reached around the back of his seat and tapped on her arm. "Rise and shine."

Yasmine yawned and rubbed the sleep out of her eyes, but somehow the short nap had actually left her feeling a bit worse. It had to be the painkillers wearing off. "Do we have any water left?" Noel passed her his bottle with a few gulps left, and she took her next dose of pills.

He opened the back door for her, and she climbed out. "Where are we?"

They'd pulled into the driveway of a home with a wide, untamed lawn. It looked like an upper-middle-class suburb, except that none of the homes were in very good shape. The driveways were empty of vehicles, including the driveway they'd pulled into.

"It's an FBI safe house," Noel explained. "Crais wanted to meet here instead of at the FBI office, and I wasn't about to ask him to drive all the way to Newherst."

"Why didn't he want to meet at the office?" Yasmine couldn't stop looking up and down the street. Where were all the people?

"This place seems completely deserted. Like a ghost town."

Noel shrugged. "I don't know, but I'm sure he has a good reason. And I assume this is one of the abandoned areas in Buffalo. Detroit has neighborhoods like this, too, but both cities are starting to revitalize some neighborhoods thanks to dirt-cheap real estate. The instability in so many cities these days makes me glad to call a small town like Newherst home, even if I haven't lived there for a while."

"No kidding. Is your mentor here?" Noel looked up at the house in front of them with a confidence that Yasmine didn't share. The whole situation felt off. "I guess the lack of traffic means we'll hear anyone coming, but it makes more sense to me to meet at the FBI office."

Noel started up the red brick path that led to a set of unkempt stone porch steps. "This isn't officially an FBI investigation yet, remember? We need to hash out the details on how to make it one before the military steps in and tries to take over. They'll shut us out and it could be years before you get answers about Daniel."

"If you say so."

At the door, Noel knocked three times, waited and then knocked once more.

"Secret code?" she asked.

He gave her a quizzical look. "Courtesy."

Within seconds, footsteps thudded inside the house. A latch turned, and the door opened to reveal a dark-haired man in a black suit. His short, spiked hair and manicured goatee reminded Yasmine of a television character, though she couldn't recall exactly whom.

"Black?"

Noel held up his badge. "The same. Special Agent Crais?"

Crais opened the door wider and gestured them inside. He shut and locked it behind them. "Down the hall to the right. Take a seat if you like."

Yasmine followed Noel, her sense of unease growing by the minute. All of the blinds were closed. The house had sparse decor, and all the furniture and carpets were black or dark brown. As they entered a moderate-size living room, she noticed a layer of dust coating a side table. Did the FBI not pay to keep up their properties?

"It's good to finally meet you, sir, but if you don't mind, I'll get right to it." Noel stood rather than taking a seat. Crais stepped into the room behind them and clasped his hands

at his front. "If the local police or even just
the captain has been taking payouts from this
inspection facility, we've got a big problem.
There's no question there. But I've no idea
how the soldier who was supposed to have
been killed in action fits into this. It doesn't
make sense."

Crais nodded slowly, rolling his shoulders
back. His movements were calculated. Deliberate. "You're right. It's a mess. But what
makes you think someone is receiving payouts from this inspection facility? What
makes you think it's not just the work of a
corrupt manager? Maybe he's just greedy."

"A greedy manager who has enough money
and organizational skills to launch a series
of coordinated attacks on Miss Browder?"
Yasmine waved at Crais, who nodded his ac-
knowledgment. Noel continued. "I mean, the
guy definitely has money, but there's absolutely no way he's behind these attacks. I had
time to think on the way over here, and I'm
wondering—what if this goes higher? What
if there's a chain of corruption that goes beyond the facility? It would explain the attacks
and the dead soldier who turned out to be
very much alive. Only someone with extensive reach, resources and considerable cash
flow could have recruited a soldier and con-

vinced him to fake his death, since that's what this is looking like with our current information. There's got to be somebody at the top making calls, somebody who has money and authority and power, and who for whatever reason believes that Daniel Browder's sister also knew about these falsified reports. And they're trying to cover their tracks."

Yasmine stared at Noel. His face was flushed and his eyes bright, and for one inexplicable instant she wanted nothing more than for him to sweep her off her feet and kiss her with the same intensity he'd given to making that speech. But when she looked over at Crais to see his reaction, the intensity was of quite a different kind. Darker.

"You're assuming that these falsified reports exist and that they're the cause of the attacks. Without proof, it's going to be extremely difficult to pursue that line of thinking."

"But—"

Crais held up a hand. "I'm not saying you're wrong. Only that it's going to be difficult, and you can't rule out anything yet, even the local police."

Noel seemed to shrink under his mentor's scrutiny. "I know. That's why I was hoping you'd know a way to open an investigation and convince a judge to give us a warrant to subpoena the facility's documents, the manager's emails, financials, whatever it takes. This is about more than one man's death. If it really is a case of falsified inspection reports, we could be sending soldiers out into the field with shoddy equipment, pieces that aren't up to standard and could fail on them in a critical moment. That'll cost more than one life. And if it goes higher? I mean, if there's a Department of Defense connection, or other government service—"

"Stop." Crais grunted and shook his head. "I don't want to hear any more."

"I don't understand."

Crais's sigh was heavy. "I should say, I don't want to *know* any more, for your sake and mine. Black, I didn't ask you to come here to talk only about this situation. I've received an official request from the Department of Defense to detain Miss Browder and pull you in early to the Buffalo office."

Yasmine's stomach dropped. Her gaze flicked to the standard-issue Glock holstered on Crais's belt, the same kind of gun that Noel had strapped to him right now, making her the only unarmed person in the room despite being able to use a weapon as well as these men. Maybe better.

She inched closer to Noel until her right side was positioned behind him, hidden from Crais's view. Her feeling of unease wasn't going away, and she wanted to be ready to act if this meeting turned sour.

"Who made the request?" Noel demanded.

"No idea. The communication came through a secure channel from the Department of Defense, so it's definitely legitimate, but no one over there is talking. I'm getting stonewalled."

"They won't tell you anything at all? Not a clue?" Yasmine crept even closer to Noel's side, her hand snaking around his back.

"All I've been told is that it's a matter of national security." He held up his hand as Noel began to sputter in protest. "Trust me, I tried to talk to my superiors, but all I'm getting is a recommendation that I comply. In the FBI's view, there's no good reason not to. The FBI works hard to ensure we maintain a good working relationship between our organizations. Until we have a solid reason to open a case, the FBI sees no good reason for me to refuse this request."

"I can give you a few," Noel said, his words sharp.

Yasmine's fingers brushed the leather of Noel's gun holster, then slid across the bumpy ridges of the weapon's grip. With her free hand, she clutched her ribcage and leaned toward Noel to help disguise her movements as simply those of an injured victim. Yasmine froze as Noel stiffened, unsure whether he'd done so as a reaction to Crais's words or if he'd noticed that the belt around his waist was becoming lighter as she slowly slid the gun from its holster.

"If I don't follow orders, the situation worsens for both of us," Crais said.

"So, this is it?" Noel's tone grew colder. "You know something big is happening and you're still going to bring us in?"

Crais looked hard at Noel, then reached his hand inside his jacket. "In a manner of speaking."

She had to act now, before Crais pulled his own weapon from inside his jacket and things turned messy. In one smooth move, Yasmine drew Noel's gun the rest of the way, straightened and trained it on the FBI agent in front of them. "Not if we can help it."

NINE

"Whoa! Hold on, Miss Browder." With excruciating slowness, Crais withdrew his hand from his jacket. He held up a phone—not a gun. Noel released the breath he'd been holding and waved at her to stand down.

"Yasmine? He's not going to kill us or turn us in. Right?" The tension in the room was so tight Noel feared it might snap at any moment.

Crais's attention slipped from Yasmine and the gun back to Noel, a hint of a strained smile in the corner of his mouth. "Make it look convincing, Black. My hands are tied, but you're not technically on the clock for another five days. I'll let you follow the breadcrumbs, and I'll have your back where I can, but I'll also need to play along with the Department of Defense as much as possible to buy time for you to figure out what's going on." He shifted his attention to Yasmine again. "Sufficient, Miss Browder?"

For a moment, Noel feared she might not believe him—that she still suspected a double-cross—but she lowered the gun and nodded. "As long as you follow through, yes."

Noel opened his palm again, but Yasmine still clung to the weapon. "You'll have to give the Department of Defense a reason we're not in custody, and it'll need to be believable."

Crais waved the phone. "I'm expecting a call at any moment to confirm that I've detained you both. If I answer, I'll have to lie, and I can't do that. If I don't answer, you'll have only a few minutes before reinforcements arrive."

"What should we do?" Yasmine's voice remained steady, to Noel's surprise. If she felt as anxious as he did, she didn't show it.

"You're going to take my car keys so that I can't be coerced into going after you," Crais said, pulling a set of keys out of his pocket. He tossed them to Noel. "And then you're going to knock me out."

"Sir?"

"Based on what you've told me so far, Black, this is a life-or-death scenario. If I'm going to be any help to you on the inside, there can't be any suspicion cast my way. I need to appear one hundred percent compliant with Department of Defense requests."

Noel felt sick to his stomach. "But it'll look like we assaulted a federal agent." If they didn't figure out what was going on, that action alone would end Noel's career before he'd even started it. His hands began to shake as the consequences of what they had to do sank in.

And then Yasmine was beside him, touching his arm. "It's okay. I won't let you put your future, your career on the line. I'll do it."

"Yasmine, no." He couldn't ask that of her. Crais cleared his throat, and Noel stared at his mentor. "You, too?"

"If this comes back to either of you, an experienced lawyer can claim self-defense for her, whereas you'd lose your job before you checked in for your first day."

Noel groaned and pressed the heels of his palms against his eyes. "This can't be happening."

"But it is," Yasmine said. "It's all right, Noel. I'll do it."

"Time's up," Crais said, his voice rising. As soon as the words left his mouth, the trill of a cell phone ring cut through the silence of the safe house. "It's my contact."

Noel met Yasmine's gaze and tilted his head. She nodded once in return and strode forward while Crais tossed his phone across the room as though he'd lost it in a struggle. Noel watched, overcome by a sense of helplessness as Yasmine used a curtain tie to secure Crais's hands behind his back. As she stood up, his mentor met his gaze.

"Be careful," he said. "This is big, Black. You make it through this and you'll be the most promising recruit I've ever had the honor of mentoring. I'm sorry you were thrown into the fire before you'd even started, but I'll do what I can from the inside."

Before Noel could verbally extend his gratitude, Yasmine had drawn her arm back, still standing behind Crais. He realized what she meant to do only in the moment that his Glock swung down and across the side of Crais's head. It connected with a loud thwack and the man fell over, unconscious.

Noel couldn't stop his shout of alarm, but he also knew that Yasmine had only done what she needed to in order to protect both his and Crais's careers in the FBI.

She extended the gun back to Noel. Her eyes were red and filled with sadness, but no tears fell. "We should get out of here. The phone isn't ringing anymore, and Crais said we'd have only minutes to exit the place before reinforcements are sent in."

Noel nodded, surprised to feel a strange

veil of calm settling over his shoulders. Nothing was as it seemed. All he'd wanted to do was make a difference in this world, and now he'd stumbled onto something big and terrifying and totally beyond his abilities or training. But Crais believed in him, and that was the encouragement he needed to keep moving forward.

Plus, whatever came next, he wasn't going to have to face it alone.

"Ready to run?" he asked, looking at the motionless body of his FBI mentor.

Yasmine sighed, sounding as though the events of the day had caught up with her. He didn't blame her one bit. She crossed the room, then pulled back the edge of the curtains to look outside for a moment before dropping them back into place. "Let's go."

They left the house, moving as quickly as they could back to Noel's mom's car. Yasmine climbed into the front passenger seat.

Noel scowled at her. "What are you doing? Get back there and lie down."

"You're going to need an extra set of eyes, right? I can endure a little bit of pain for that."

Noel shook his head and muttered under his breath. He reversed the car and pulled out of the driveway. They made it less than a block before he hit the brakes. "You see what I'm seeing?"

Yasmine squinted down the long residential road and groaned. A vehicle drove toward them, big enough to be a black SUV like the one that had smashed into them. "Reverse. Now."

"Already on it."

Here in this deserted subdivision, anything could happen, and it'd be a long time before anyone found out about it. Yasmine gripped her seat as Noel reversed and pulled back into the driveway.

"What are you doing?" She gaped at him. Had he lost his mind?

"We have Crais's keys, so his car must be around here somewhere." He climbed out of his mom's car, and Yasmine followed him as he ran back toward the house. He fiddled with the gate latch to the backyard. "Come on, come on."

Moments later, he pulled the gate open, and they dashed through.

"Uh, Noel?" Yasmine heard the sound of an engine drawing closer. They'd definitely run out of time. "I doubt Crais parked his car in the backyard, considering it's fenced in and that's therefore impossible."

"True, but I have a strong hunch we'll find

the yard connects to the neighbor's place on the other side." He shut the gate behind him and surveyed the yard, which was fenced in with no sign of an exit save for the gate they'd entered through. They were trapped, but Noel held a finger to his lips and raced across the grass. Yasmine's heart lurched into her throat at the crackle of tires rolling onto a driveway.

"Noel?" she whispered as loud as she could without giving away their position. Slamming doors and pounding feet told her that they were seconds away from being discovered. If anyone moved to the back of the house and looked out the blinds, they'd be seen.

Noel ran his hands along the back fence, one on their side and one overtop on the neighbor's side. His face grew tighter and tighter until he stopped his forward motion. He waved her over with the barest hint of a smile.

Did she dare? Maybe they could wait until all of the people in the vehicle got out, then run through the front of the house and hi- jack the SUV— No, what was she thinking? It might be risky without cracked ribs and a body covered in bruises, but considering her injuries, it'd be impossible. She walked as fast as she could to where Noel yanked at something on the other side of the fence. He pushed on the slats in front of him. A second gate swung open, perfectly positioned along the fence to hide that it was there at all.

She slipped through and he followed, closing the gate and latching it at the same moment the glass patio door at the back of the house slid open. Noel held his finger to his lips, but Yasmine's heart pounded a nearly deafening rhythm inside her chest. It was a wonder that that alone hadn't given away their position.

A walkie-talkie beeped near the house, and Yasmine heard the crackle of garbled instructions through the device's speaker. Seconds later, the glass door slid closed.

Noel held up three fingers and counted them down, lowering his fingers one by one. She shook her head. Did he remember that she couldn't run?

Three. Two. One.

On one, Noel ran across the neighbor's yard in a crouch, moving along the edge of the fence. Yasmine moved along the same path, but crouching was out of the question. When they reached the front of the house, Noel stood in the driveway, hands on his hips. He looked stumped.

"What did you expect to find?" Yasmine took in this new street. It looked more or less the same as the one they'd come from. "Are we holing up inside one of these places, or...?"

Noel glanced down the street again. "No. I thought we'd find Crais's car. It's a tactic to avoid detection, park on the other side of the fence. There's a house and fence set up similar to this in Hogan's Alley."

"Hogan's Alley?"

"Yeah, the tactical training facility at the FBI Academy."

Yasmine pointed at the garage. "Would he have parked it in there?"

Noel's smile sent a rush of warmth to Yasmine's cheeks. Wordlessly he reached for the bottom of the garage door and bent his knees to raise it. The door resisted for a moment before sliding up, creaking with the sound of equipment left to decay. Yasmine winced at the noise. If anyone had been outside at the safe house, there was no way they'd have missed hearing that.

Sure enough, a shiny black Suburban sat inside the garage. Noel dug inside his pocket and pulled out Crais's keys. He unlocked the doors and they climbed inside. Then he started the vehicle and pulled onto the street. "It figures. We're going to have to stop for gas soon. I'll do what I can to maximize mileage until we find a station that's safe to pull into."

Yasmine heard the tension in his voice, the effort to keep panic and fear from taking over.

"And there goes our lead." He adjusted the rearview mirror and growled, "They heard us."

Of course they had. The past two days had been nothing but a nightmare that showed no sign of stopping. Yasmine watched in the side mirror as another black SUV similar to the one they sat in pulled onto the street, closing the gap between them even as Noel increased their speed.

Within seconds, an arm snaked out the passenger side of the SUV. A gun aimed toward her and Noel as the distance that separated the vehicles grew slimmer.

For the first time since all of this had begun, a stark truth hit Yasmine right between the eyes.

They weren't going to make it.

TEN

"Hold on." Noel pounded the gas pedal and shifted gears. Yasmine grew strangely quiet. Was she all right? She'd pistol-whipped Crais in the head without an ounce of hesitation. She'd certainly learned a thing or two in the military, and her compartmentalization—while helpful in the heat of the moment—had to overload eventually. She'd been keeping her emotions in check for almost the entire time since he'd reunited with her yesterday. Had it really been only twenty-four hours since this madness had begun? It felt as though they'd been dodging bullets for a week.

A crack split the air, and the back windshield crunched. Two more shots slammed into the vehicle, but the window held. Like his own car, the Suburban had bulletproof glass—one of the advantages of commandeering an FBI vehicle.

Noel shot through the next intersection,

pulling onto a main road. Few other cars traveled the street, but it led to a major highway that would take them out of Buffalo's suburbs and back toward Newherst.

"I'm going to try to lose them on back roads," Noel said, gritting his teeth for the next turn. He waited until the last second to yank the wheel to the left, not bothering to signal or step on the brakes. He hoped the driver following them would overshoot the turn or at least be blocked for a few seconds while the oncoming wave of vehicles passed by.

Instead, their pursuers turned directly into oncoming traffic. The screech of brakes told Noel that he'd misjudged the recklessness of the pursuing driver. He mentally kicked himself. He'd thought it would be FBI potentially coming after them, but the driver wasn't acting like FBI—Noel knew the typical maneuvers inside and out after twenty weeks at the Academy. Had someone co-opted Crais's instructions or taken over the recovery operation? It made sense. The people after Yasmine always knew where she'd be, and the Department of Defense had the pull and resources to take over a recovery operation—even without giving Crais or his superiors all the information. Noel couldn't believe he'd forgotten to consider all the angles. He needed to up his game, because if the driver behind them was cut from the same cloth as the sniper who'd committed suicide rather than allow himself to be caught, of course he'd put himself at risk to get the job done.

"The ride is going to get a little rough," Noel said, pressing the gas pedal again as he turned onto a side street. "Hold on. If your ribs hurt, let me know, but I'm afraid it's escape or risk one of those bullets in our backs."

"It's okay," Yasmine said. "Do what you need to do."

Her words were strangely reassuring. He snuck a glance at her. She stared forward at the road ahead, occasionally looking in the side mirror to check on their pursuers. How had she grown up to be even more beautiful than he remembered? And what on earth was a woman like her doing unattached and living with her brother in a tiny town like Newherst? When he looked at her, he saw a woman who could do anything she wanted, achieve whatever she set her mind to. She'd be a handful for any man trying to love her, but he had no doubt it would bring a lifetime of rewards. Of adventure.

Life never had a dull moment with Yasmine Browder, he'd told her when they were kids. He'd meant it in a teasing way back then, but now...

Another crack against the back windshield sent him spinning out of his thoughts. The last thing he needed was to get shot again—the last time it happened, his career on the police force had effectively been ended.

"Where are you, Black? Back to earth, please." Yasmine pulled out her cell phone and ran her thumb across the back of its case. "Isn't there anyone else we can call? Somebody who might be able to help us?"

Noel wished there was, but Crais's words had thrown everything into doubt. "I don't know. I'm still not sure we can trust the police, and we can't go to the FBI, lest we risk compromising Crais. Who could possibly be trying to give orders to a top-ranking FBI agent?"

"Somebody who knows how to manipulate the system. Who knew that Crais would have his hands tied by needing to follow protocol. Someone who has both the money and leverage to make this work."

Noel veered right at the next road, taking them onto the highway. The red glow of the setting sun reflected in his mirror. Could they lose their pursuers before dark? He had to start thinking of their solution for the night ahead. Yasmine needed to rest and recover tonight. Her injuries would never heal if her body kept taking on stress.

"I'm not sure how that helps us," he said, distracted as the SUV behind them raced up the ramp, following them onto the highway. It was only a matter of time before city police or state troopers joined the chase, too—after all, their pursuers had fired shots from the vehicle in a populated area.

"Noel, I'm going to blame your denseness on the stress of the moment."

"I'm grateful?"

"You should be." The glow of her smile gifted him with a slight diffusion of anxiety in the heat of the moment. "We need to follow the money. That's the only way we're going to figure this out."

Of course. "But how are we going to do that? I can't ask for a subpoena of records, not now. And if Crais does it, he'll be put in danger or end up under serious scrutiny, and then we'll lose our inside man."

Plus, they'd assaulted a federal agent—with permission, but the FBI didn't know that. What the consequences were for the both of them until this situation got resolved, he wasn't sure—but he didn't want to worry Yasmine over it.

"Did you have anyone from the cyber division in your graduating class at the academy?"

"It's illegal for the FBI to hack into someone's financials without a warrant. We can't do that. Private citizens can get more information with an online search and a credit card than the Bureau can these days. You just have to know where to look."

"Do *you* know where to look?"

Noel shook his head. One name had popped into his head, and though it might be a long shot, the person definitely was not corrupt. "First we're going to lose these goons behind us. Then we're going to call my uncle in Pennsylvania."

"Your uncle? What does he have to do with any of this?"

"Personally? Nothing." His uncle, Chief Walter Black, had been on the police force for a very long time and had connections the likes of which it would take Noel an entire career to build. "But I'm hoping he knows someone who can help us."

It was more than a long shot. More like a futile hope in the impossible.

Given the choice between running forever and the impossible, though? He glanced at the woman next to him, battered and bruised and exhausted thanks to the work of those who believed themselves above the law.

He'd gladly put his hope in the impossible if it meant any chance, no matter how small, at getting Yasmine out of this mess.

Yasmine held her breath as Noel maneuvered their Suburban like a professional. He dodged and weaved to keep them out of harm's way, but with every crack and bang against the vehicle, she grew more and more fearful that they wouldn't be able to lose their tail before their pursuers managed a few decent shots at their tires. Who were these people? Even Noel looked nervous every time he glanced in the rearview mirror.

At the next straightaway, Noel pressed the pedal to the floor, and the Suburban jumped forward. There were no other vehicles nearby on this stretch, and there was a hill up ahead. Yasmine wondered if Noel had a plan or if he intended only to put distance between them and the armed assailants.

"You know what you're doing? Or what's over that hill?" She looked out her window as they passed a sign for Mill River.

His jaw tightened. "If I remember correctly, there's a bridge over Mill River on the other side of the hill. The road curves after the river, so they won't have a long-distance view down the road if we can get far enough ahead."

"Ahead to what?" Yasmine realized that she hadn't heard the crack of a bullet against the vehicle for almost two minutes. When she looked in the side mirror, she saw that the car in pursuit had fallen behind. "Are you going to lose them on the hills and turns?"

"No. We're going to stop running. Brace yourself."

"Wait, what?" Yasmine pressed her hands against the sides of her seat as Noel shot over the crest of the hill. The vehicle came down hard with a thump that rattled her already aching bones. She really needed another painkiller, but she'd forgotten them inside Noel's mom's car back at the FBI safe house. Not good. Neither was the speed at which they descended the hill toward the bridge. "Noel, I don't think—"

Her words were cut short as, just before they reached the bridge railing, Noel yanked on the steering wheel and pulled the Suburban off-road and into the brush. The vehicle bounced and jostled, but he kept their course steady. She had no idea what was going through his head as he plunged their SUV into the shallow river and veered underneath the bridge before cutting the engine.

Yasmine hardly dared to breathe. "What did you just do?"

Noel glanced in the mirrors and drew his gun. "I used our momentum to ensure that we wouldn't stop moving once we hit the water. Listen."

Over the soft swishing of the shallow river, she heard the hum of tires coming closer. "Are we going to be able to move again if it turns out they saw us?"

"The river will come up only to your knees. It's not deep and doesn't reach the engine. But if they saw us drop in here or notice the tire tracks right before the bridge, moving will be the least of our worries. I think I waited long enough to get us off the road, so they'll be moving too quickly at the bottom of the hill to notice any scuffing."

She listened again, praying that their pursuers would keep moving. *Please, Lord. Shelter us.* The vehicle zoomed past overhead and kept going. *Thank You, God.* "Now we move?"

Noel reholstered his gun. "We'll get out of here and go back the way we came. I want to take the first road off this straightaway. Ideally by the time they realize we've given them the slip, we'll be long gone."

He started up the vehicle and rolled out

from under the bridge, getting them back on the road and over the hill in a matter of seconds. The adrenaline of running for their lives had kept the ache of her injuries at bay for the past few hours, but as minutes ticked past without a sign of their pursuers, the pain returned in a steady rush as the rest of her body began to relax.

"I forgot my medication in your mom's car," she said softly as Noel took another turn. He appeared to be heading toward a main highway. "I'm not sure what to do."

Noel grimaced and pounded the steering wheel with the heel of his palm. "I can't believe I didn't think of that. Are you going to be all right?" When she didn't respond—she didn't want to lie to him—he grunted in frustration. "We already need to find a gas station before the tank runs out and forces us into a bad situation. One of us can run inside and grab off-the-shelf painkillers while the other fills the tank. Should take three minutes, tops. I know that's not the same as your prescription, but it'll have to do. I don't want you passing out from pain during an already tense situation."

"I know." Yasmine took shallow breaths as the pain intensified. "Sooner is better, please."

Yasmine's next breath caught as Noel

glanced at her. The anguish in his eyes rivaled her own. Did he really care so much, or was he worried only about his future with the FBI? He reached across the center console and took her hand, squeezing it twice before letting go as though he'd thought better of it, like he feared he'd crossed an invisible boundary.

And he had. They were old friends, caught in the crossfire of a bizarre and mysterious operation, pushed into this position together by circumstance alone. That was the truth. That's what she believed.

So why did a part of her yearn for him to take her hand once more?

ELEVEN

Noel pulled into the gas station with his head pounding. The vehicle was running on fumes, ready to sputter and die at any moment. He'd remembered there was a gas station and rest stop just off the main highway—and though he knew stopping might be a risk, the alternative was to have the SUV run out of juice in the middle of nowhere. He pulled up to the gas pump farthest from the road, using the other vehicles at the station as scant cover.

He pulled out his phone to make the call to his uncle, Chief Walter Black, who picked up on the first ring. "Noel? Is that my big-shot FBI nephew calling all the way from Quantico?"

"Hey, Uncle Walter." His uncle sounded so excited to hear from him. He hated to be the bearer of bad news. "Graduated a few days ago, actually. I'm back in New York for a visit before starting work on Monday. But that's not why I'm calling."

"No? Well, I'm proud of you. Going federal isn't an easy job, but if anyone is cut out for it, you are."

Noel swallowed hard. He'd thought that Uncle Walter might harbor some bitterness over Noel's decision to leave the police force after taking a bullet to the leg during his second year on the job. He'd gone on medical leave and never returned. The lengthy recovery period had meant the only job he was fit for during recovery was a desk position—and so, out of frustration and by choice, he and the police force had amicably parted ways. His uncle had even vouched for him on his FBI application several years later, after he'd fully healed, but he still occasionally wondered if Uncle Walter remained a tad upset that Noel had quit police work.

"Uncle Walter, I'm going to cut right to the heart of why I'm calling as I don't have a lot of time. I'm in trouble, and I'm hoping you can help."

His uncle's jovial tone turned serious. "Go on, son."

Noel explained the situation as his uncle listened. When he came to the part about his

FBI mentor telling him to pursue the case off the books, Chief Black sighed.

"This sounds incredibly dangerous, son. You sure you can handle it?"

"I can. I know I can. I didn't endure police academy and twenty weeks of training at the FBI Academy for nothing. The issue I'm running into now, though, is that we need to access emails and financials for the facility manager, and I have no way to get to them. Because of what's happening with Crais, there's no way he can subpoena those records, and I can't get to them any other way. I was hoping…well, that you'd know a guy."

The silence on the other end sent Noel's stomach into a tailspin. If they had no way to check out those records, they'd be sunk. They had no actionable proof on anything right now, nothing to go on. They'd be dodging bullets until Yasmine took one in the back and the FBI had him locked down. Or jailed for assault. But did he really want to bring his uncle into this?

"I'm sorry, uncle. This was a bad idea. I shouldn't be taking advantage of you this way."

"Taking advantage?" Now his uncle did sound angry. "Listen up. Not only are we related, but also you're law enforcement, same as me. Who's going to have our backs if we don't help each other out? You're my people and I'm yours. This is what we do for each other. And it just so happens that I do know a guy, but you might not like it."

Noel's sudden surge of hope paused in its ascent. "Why not? What do you mean?"

"I mean…you can't ask questions. About any of it." Noel heard his uncle drum his fingers on the desktop. "I can call in a favor. Met a guy years back. Did him a solid. He promised me one favor, no questions asked, anytime I need it."

Now Noel felt really bad. "Sounds important. You might need it someday."

"Son, someday is today. Your life and the life of your friend are on the line. I'd say that's worth calling it in. Might be that God intended I cross paths with that fellow for just such a time as this."

God? Noel had never heard his uncle talk about God before. "I don't want to put you at risk."

His uncle laughed gruffly. "We're all at risk in this business. Every single day. And if I can't do something to help my favorite nephew catch the bad guys and save the girl, then I'd be a pretty terrible uncle. And let's face it. If I don't do this and something happens to you, I'll never forgive myself."

Noel swallowed the lump in his throat. He and his uncle had never been particularly close, but he understood. Family helped family. Law enforcement types looked out for their own. If the situation was reversed and his uncle phoned him for help, he'd do the same in a heartbeat.

"Okay," he said, giving in. "Call in the favor. And then tell me what I need to do."

Yasmine watched as a battle played out across Noel's features. She'd begun to feel nauseated by the pain, but they desperately needed to determine a game plan, a way to try to wrest back some control over the situation.

Noel hung up and placed his phone on the dashboard. "We're going to get another phone call in a few minutes," he said, his expression as serious as she'd ever seen it. "I'll do the talking, but I'm going to put it on speaker so you can hear."

He looked across the row of gas pumps and then at her. Her heart lurched, and clenched her hands into fists to quell the nervous tension. "Listen, when the guy calls, don't say anything, all right?"

That didn't sound good, but she nodded her agreement. "Is this, uh, aboveboard?"

Noel pressed his lips together and ran his fingers through his hair. "I don't want to ask those questions. In fact, we're not allowed to ask those questions. I have a feeling that in the United States, it might not be considered aboveboard, but my uncle has called in a favor from someone who can hack into things for us, and he doesn't seem bothered by it. My uncle's a good man. He wouldn't knowingly break the law. That means whoever he's calling in a favor from is either a civilian or..." He stopped before he said it, but Yasmine could put two and two together.

"CIA?" she whispered. "An agent stationed outside of the United States?"

Noel didn't say anything but looked at her pointedly. They sat for what seemed like an eternity, waiting and keeping watch. Yasmine's stomach churned in anticipation and her head spun. What if the people after her found them before the call came in? What if Noel's uncle wasn't able to get in touch with his contact?

She was about to suggest they fill up the gas tank while they waited when the phone buzzed.

Noel reached for the phone and swiped to accept the call. "Noel Black here, FBI."

"Good evening, Special Agent Black. My name is Shaun." The caller paused as if choosing his next words very carefully. "I understand you're in search of some sensitive information that is, let's say, difficult for you to obtain with your current credentials."

Yasmine swallowed, her throat suddenly dry. Shaun sounded friendly enough, at least, but the whole situation was nerve-racking.

"That's correct," Noel said. Yasmine noticed that his hands had balled into fists, which he squeezed every few seconds like a pulse. "Did my uncle explain the situation to you?"

"He did. Financial records for Anthony Clarke, manager of a military equipment inspection facility contracted by the Department of Defense. Those were easy. The local police, not so much, because I had to look past the public records. I will say this, however. I didn't notice anything strange with the police records. Your facility manager, that's another story."

Yasmine caught Noel's eye and rolled her index fingers around each other. She wanted Noel to keep Shaun talking, but to do it quickly. They'd already spent too much time here. Noel nodded, already on board.

"And?" Noel said.

"I'm going to send to you what I found in a digital format, secured on a cloud storage account. I'll also send details on how to access the account, because you'll want to see this for yourself and then decide what to do with it."

"Of course." Noel's fists squeezed again. "Something to be concerned about, I take it?"

"I'm no special agent, but it looks fishy. Anthony Clarke has been receiving financial handouts from an offshore account at what looks like a dummy corporation. The good news is that I've seen this kind of thing before. However, this one was hidden extremely well. Want to take a stab at who it belongs to?"

Noel's face went blank, but Yasmine's mind screamed an answer. When Noel didn't speak up, Yasmine did. Noel visibly flinched as she ignored his instructions not to speak. "It's got to be the Department of Defense. There's no other explanation, but at the same time, it hardly makes sense."

"You got it. Miss Browder, I take it?"

"Yes, sir. Can you tell who set it up?" Yasmine touched Noel's shoulder. He still hadn't reacted to Shaun's information, but neither had he stopped her from interjecting into the conversation. If anything, he looked mildly relieved.

"I'm still trying, but I don't think I'm going to be able to break through the security in front of the information without tipping off the person who set it up. I can't give you a name, but at least you know that someone at the Department of Defense isn't playing by the rules. This trail is telling me that there's untested military equipment being rushed into the field to advance quota and receive a bigger financial payout from the Department. The money then moves from the inspection facility and back to this Department of Defense shell account, which pays out a portion of that to Anthony Clarke."

Noel slammed his fist on the steering wheel. "Those unethical, heartless——"

"Huh." Shaun's voice came through the line again, hesitant.

"What is it?" Noel growled, then sighed. "Sorry. I shouldn't shoot the messenger. I'm just frustrated."

"I understand. You're not going to like this either, so brace yourself."

"Tell me."

"There's a second account that's also receiving payouts from the shell account. But

I can't hack it. Can't trace it, can't see into it, can't tell anything about it except that… wow. Wow."

"Shaun." Noel came dangerously close to growling at their contact again. Yasmine touched his shoulder, trying to calm him down. If he annoyed the man doing them a favor, they'd be back to square one. They needed him on their side. The tension in Noel's shoulders eased with Yasmine's touch, but only slightly.

"I know, I know." More silence. More typing. "These payouts to the second account? They're massive. Much, much bigger than what Clarke is receiving. That facility is moving a lot of untested parts, putting thousands of American soldiers at risk. There's no other way there could be this much money going into the second account. I wish I could see who it's for, but I'm blind here."

"How much money?" Yasmine spoke before Noel could. "Can you see that, at least?"

On the other end of the line, Shaun grew silent. Moments later, his words were strained. "Millions. Whoever's on the receiving end of that second account is getting millions from the shell account. The Department of Defense isn't supposed to work like that. They're federally accountable for their finances. Wherever this money is going, someone over there doesn't want anyone to know about it. And that can't be anything good."

TWELVE

Moments later, they ended the call with Shaun, thanking him for his willingness to assist them. Shaun promised to send the cloud storage account information as soon as they were off the phone, but reminded them that now that they had this information about what appeared to be incredibly corrupt financial reporting at the Department of Defense, it would be up to them to figure out what to do with it.

Yasmine had an idea of her own, but she wasn't sure that Noel would go for it. It was risky, but at the same time, it was the only option she could think of that wouldn't end with them staring down the barrel of yet another gun.

"Thoughts?" she asked. "I know what I want to do, but you're FBI. Let's hear your plan first."

He ran his hand down the side of his face.

"I see only one way out of this, Yasmine. And I don't think you're going to like it. I really don't."

"Try me."

He raked his eyes across her features as if searching for some falsehood in her words and tone. "I'm not joking."

"Neither am I. Noel, we've been shot at, my brother is dead and even your FBI mentor is worried. This is no time to hedge your thoughts. Spit it out."

He nodded and slipped his phone into his pocket. "You're right. In that case, since we don't know who else we can trust, I say we go straight to the source."

"The Department of Defense," Yasmine and Noel said at the same time.

Noel stared at her in surprise as Yasmine continued. "I agree. That was going to be my suggestion, too. Shaun said that the Department doesn't typically behave this way, that they report federally just like any other government organization. There's no way the entire Department knows about this, so there must be a few select individuals who've set this all up. I can't even begin to guess where that amount of money is going, but if we take this paper trail information directly to the source as evidence—"

"—they'll have to act. They're not going to want this to continue or get out to the public. Could you imagine the damage that would do? The American public and the world's media would skin the administration alive. Not to mention that millions of dollars funneling into a mystery account is terrifying enough. That could be going anywhere, to anyone. And that much secrecy—"

"—is worrying. Really, really worrying." Yasmine rested her head against the back of the seat. "So, now what?"

Noel tapped the keys. "We fill up the tank and go to the Pentagon."

"You want to drive all the way there?"

"You have a better idea? We've lost our tail, and I'm not willing to risk us being cornered on a bus or train. I know you're in no shape to drive, so I'll manage it."

"Noel, the Pentagon is seven hours away."

"We have no other choice. Wait here. When we're full, I'm going to pay cash. I doubt anyone is monitoring our cards, but it's a needless risk." He slipped out the door, and Yasmine closed her eyes as Noel pumped the gas. *God, give us strength.* Seven hours in a car with Noel? He'd be exhausted by the time they made it to DC, but she agreed with his logic. Better to drive there and control the situation the whole time than risk being located and found on public transportation. It also put fewer civilians in the potential path of danger.

As Noel walked toward the station kiosk to pay, Yasmine leaned back in her seat again… and played back Noel's words about credit card tracking. They couldn't be too careful, sure, and yet here they were inside an FBI vehicle. *Government vehicles are traceable.*

Without a wasted second, Yasmine exited her side of the Suburban and crossed to the driver's side. She opened the door and gingerly crawled onto the floor before flipping onto her back so that her legs dangled out the driver's side while she stared up into the inner workings of the vehicle.

She scanned the dark mess of wires, looking for anything out of place. She wasn't great with cars in general, but identifying and disabling a tracker was a basic military skill— and there it was, a small box about half the size of a paperback book attached to the inside of the dash. Aftermarket GPS trackers were effective but not complicated devices. She wrapped her fingers around it and pulled.

"Need any help there, miss?"

Yasmine sat up in surprise and nearly smacked her head. A middle-aged man stood by the vehicle, looking for all the world like he couldn't believe a lady would be able to examine the inner workings of a car all by herself.

"No, I'm fine, thank you," she began to say, but she made it only halfway through the sentence before the man blanched and backed away. He almost ran as he slunk back to his vehicle, a compact car that appeared to contain other passengers.

Weird. Yasmine lay back down. She gripped the GPS transmitter and tensed for one final tug. It came free, and she immediately ran her fingers along the edge for a switch, then thought better of it. She slid out from her place on the floor while ignoring her protesting ribs and looked up to see Noel walking too quickly back to her, his face ashen.

"We have to go." He tossed a small white bottle to her but kept his voice low as he approached. "What part of stay in the car didn't you get?"

She held up the tracker, then dumped it into the trash can next to the gas pump. "GPS. I don't recommend destroying government property, but if we leave it turned on, anyone after us will waste time coming here, and we'll be long gone."

Noel's cheeks turned a light shade of pink. "I should have thought of that."

She shrugged. "You're new. I should have thought of it earlier, too."

"Still." He motioned for her to get back inside the vehicle. "Let's move. Don't make eye contact with anyone, and keep your head down."

"Don't scare me. What is it? Have we been spotted?"

Noel's grimace betrayed his frustration. "Please trust me. I'll explain on the road, but we need to go. Now."

She didn't appreciate being told what to do, but after all they'd been through, she knew it'd be foolish not to take him at his word. With a slight nod, she rounded the vehicle, keeping her gaze lowered while trying to look inconspicuous.

She reached the door just as a man appeared from the rear, the same guy who'd asked a few minutes ago if she needed help. This time, he had a second guy with him. The first man reached toward her. "Hey, lady!"

She ignored him and pulled open the SUV door. What on earth was happening?

"Don't respond. Get in," Noel urged, already in his seat.

She tried, but the second man's arm shot

out to block her from getting inside, a mixture of fear and anger on his face. "I'm going to have to ask you to leave this woman," he said, looking over his shoulder at Noel. The lunacy of his statement almost caused Yasmine to laugh, but Noel's stiffened posture told her that would be a bad idea.

"I'm taking care of her," Noel replied, his words curt.

"Yeah? Says who? Because I say you're the one who came in here with the lady, and it was only after you arrived that the alert came up. Maybe you're helping her escape."

"Escape?" Yasmine stared at the stranger. "Listen, mister—"

Noel reached into his jacket, presumably to pull out his badge, but the stranger who'd blocked her path had diverted Noel's attention. Yasmine shouted a warning as the first man appeared at the driver's side and yanked it open to take a swing at Noel.

"What is going on?" she shouted at Noel.

"You're on TV," he grunted, still grappling with the man. "Get in! Get in!"

Yasmine looked up and saw other customers pointing at the gas pump TV displays. Her face and name were splashed across the screen—across every screen—and a red bar scrolled across the bottom of the image, decrying her as a dangerous person, wanted by the FBI.

"Oh, fantastic," she muttered. "Auntie Zee is going to kill me."

Arms suddenly closed around her neck and waist. She shouted in pain at the pressure on her ribs and reacted on instinct, grabbing the arms and shifting her weight to toss her attacker, the motion earning her another stab of pain. The man flew over her shoulder and landed in front of her with a thud. He was a citizen performing what he believed to be his civic duty, no doubt, but—

"I'm FBI!" Noel's shout stopped the men in place. He held up his badge, flashing it to the other nearby patrons and the men who'd attacked them. As news of a ten-thousand-dollar reward flashed up on screen for information leading to her arrest, Yasmine realized just how motivated these people were to make a citizen's arrest.

Yasmine climbed over the man on the ground and back into the Suburban as Noel held his badge aloft through the window.

"As soon as you tell me we're clear, we go," he said.

She checked to make sure they wouldn't run over the man on the ground, then slammed her door. "Let's get out of here."

* * *

Noel pulled out of the parking lot before Yasmine had even buckled her seat belt. Once he saw she was secured, he stepped on the gas pedal and zoomed down the road. He buckled his own seat belt at the first turn, earning a look of frustration from Yasmine.

"We had to move," he said, thinking she was upset about his delayed act of seat belt safety.

"It's not that." She sighed and thumped her head against the seat rest. "Wanted by the FBI. I thought Crais was on our side?"

"He is," Noel growled. *He has to be.* "I'm sure there's an explanation for this."

"If the explanation is that we've been double-crossed by your mentor, we're going to be in real trouble."

"He wouldn't do that." Noel focused on the road again, trying to push aside the doubts and fears that assaulted him from every side. Crais betraying them? That would mean they really didn't have anyone left to trust. There'd be no going back to the FBI, no career left for Noel after they sorted this out. Crais was too high up at the Bureau, and Noel would be a marked man for having assisted Yasmine during her escape from…whatever this was.

From whatever they'd pinned on her. "It's not possible."

Even he heard the waver in his voice.

"But why only me, Noel? I don't get it. Why don't they want you?"

That was easy to answer, and Noel felt good to be able to explain at least one thing about what they were going through. "Because the FBI doesn't want to lose face. Could you imagine putting a wanted notice out for a brand-new FBI recruit? They don't let just anyone into the Academy, and the level of scrutiny we're under during training is enormous. If they put my picture up as a wanted person, it'd be a simple process for the media to figure out I'm a new FBI special agent and get the Bureau torn apart in the media. The FBI would come out looking like an organization of fools who can't do their jobs. Makes more sense to put up your picture as a wanted person and discipline me internally once I'm back in their hands."

"Or maybe they don't blame you at all. Maybe someone got to him? Paid him off when we evaded them, to avoid us going back to him for help?"

Noel's stomach sank toward his shoes. "I guess that's possible. Plausible, even." He ran a hand down the side of his face again, wishing not for the first time that he had more experience. An FBI agent with a long history might have a better chance at outsmarting bad guys, but him? He was so green it was all he could do to keep his cool. Having Yasmine around seemed to be helping. In fact, he'd begun to wonder how he'd managed all these years without her.

So much about her had changed, yes—but in even more ways, she was still the same girl he'd had a crush on all those years ago. Only now, he felt something much deeper when he looked at her...and yet, they still had a massive wall of lost years between them.

He glanced at Yasmine, wondering if he should ask again about her time in Amar, but she'd turned to gaze out the window at the passing landscape as the sun sank the rest of the way below the horizon. He swallowed his curiosity and focused on the road. They had a long way to go and would need to form a solid plan before reaching the Pentagon. Getting inside wouldn't be easy—Noel was well aware of that—but his status as an FBI agent meant it might not be impossible.

They fell into a comfortable silence, and soon he heard the slow, steady rhythm of Yasmine's breathing. She'd taken the painkillers and fallen asleep with her head lolled against the window, one hand tucked underneath her cheek. How could she sleep like that? She'd wake with an awful cramp if she slept that way for long.

She looked so beautiful with her eyelids closed and her lips slightly parted. Her mouth was so soft, so inviting. If only they weren't running for their lives.

"Eyes on the road, Fed," Yasmine mumbled.

He flushed and stared straight ahead. He should have known better than to sneak so many looks her way. "Sorry. How's the pain?"

"Okay. I'll need to take more medicine before we reach DC."

"Got it." She sat upright and shifted in the seat, and from the corner of his eye he saw her turn toward him but then settle back in place as though she'd changed her mind about something.

After much time and many miles, Yasmine finally spoke. "Noel...I haven't told you the whole story about why I stayed away."

He swallowed the lump that immediately formed in his throat. This was what he'd been waiting to hear, but the strain in her voice made him wonder if he wanted to hear it, after all. "It's okay, Mina. You don't have to tell me."

"No, I want to." She sighed deeply and turned slightly toward him again. "I met someone in Amar."

Noel's stomach tightened. He remained silent, not wanting to spook her, because something in her tone told him that this was the thing she'd held back from him since they'd reunited. She'd been so evasive when he'd asked about Amar. He pressed his lips together to keep from blurting out his questions.

"His name was Marc. He loved computers and worked as an information technology specialist at the American University of Amar. We met while I was in school, long before I signed up for military service. It was only because of him that I enrolled. He hadn't yet done his year of compulsory service, and the only way for me to be able to remain in Amar was to obtain dual citizenship, which required completion of the compulsory service."

Noel wanted to ask why she'd wanted to become a dual citizen, but he had a feeling he knew what she'd say. His suspicions were confirmed by her next words.

"We were engaged. Immigration laws in Amar are very strict, so if I wanted to take the job offer I had, get married and stay there, dual citizenship was the only option. Turned out it was all for nothing."

Noel clenched his jaw, getting an even worse feeling about where the story was going. "What happened?"

Yasmine's tone shifted from sad to matter-of-fact. "Simply put? He cheated on me, and I only found out about it when I caught him. I thought he loved me, but it turned out I was wrong."

"Yasmine, I'm so sorry." The tension in Noel's stomach turned quickly to anger. "That's horrible. To have seen that, to have endured that kind of betrayal...I can't even imagine."

"He was an excellent liar," she said, her voice lowered to nearly a whisper. "He had me fooled, Noel. We were together for nearly five years. How many other times had he done that behind my back? I still don't know, and I don't want to. I moved back to the United States partially to escape that memory, that pain of being in the same country as him. I just couldn't be there anymore. I wanted to come home. Plus, Daniel was here, and Dad's side of the family is spread out across the East Coast. And Mom's sister is here, Auntie Zee—she came back when we didn't. Still, I'm...I'm not sure I did the right thing, sometimes. Moving back here."

Instinctively, Noel reached across the seats

and took Yasmine's hand where it rested in her lap. "You did what you had to do to move on. Marc was an idiot. Anyone who would do something like that…well…obviously never deserved you in the first place."

She sniffed as though trying to fend off tears. "I know that. In my head, I know that. But still I wonder, was there something I could have done? Was I lacking in some way? Maybe it's my fault he fell into another woman's arms. Maybe— Look, I'm sorry," she said, pulling her hand free from his. "I didn't mean to make a big deal about it. I just thought you deserved to know the whole story."

He cleared his throat, wishing not for the first time that he knew what to say. If Marc was anywhere in the near vicinity, he'd teach the man a thing or two about keeping promises. Yasmine deserved to be with someone who made her his world. He felt a strong urge to tell her, to erase that sadness from where it had settled across her features.

Noel maneuvered onto the side of the road, turned off the lights and cut the engine. "No, stop apologizing. Right now." In the moonlit darkness, he saw tears glisten on her cheeks. He had a sudden urge to kiss away each and every one of them.

He wanted her to know that what Marc did wasn't her fault, could never be her fault.

He wanted to make her whole again.

"You can't blame yourself," he said. "And I think you know that. It hurts—of course it does—but in the end, he made a choice to walk away from the promises you made to each other."

She shook her head. "Maybe I was wrong to make those promises to anyone in the first place. Maybe I'm just not worth it."

How could he explain it to her so she'd understand? Of course she was worth it. She was strong, capable, interesting. Unique. Beautiful. Driven. Everything that a man might want in a woman.

Everything *he* wanted in a woman.

Like a lightbulb illuminating the darkness, he realized a stark truth that he'd been trying to deny since the moment this woman had leaped across the hood of his car and plunged inside to escape an onslaught of bullets.

He might have spent ten years apart from Yasmine Browder, but she had never been far from his heart or mind. And that childhood crush? It had reblossomed in a short time into a deep, unconditional love.

Without thinking, he reached his hand behind her head and pulled her toward him. She pushed back, hesitant, for only a moment. Then she allowed him to draw her close.

"Worth it?" He whispered, his lips hovering a breath away from hers. "You, Yasmine Browder, are priceless."

And then, after more than a decade of waiting and dreaming about the possibility of this moment, he kissed her.

THIRTEEN

They breathed through the moment together, lips parted, as Yasmine's mind dashed from sensation to sensation. The gentleness of his touch and the comfort of his fingers entwined in her hair. The rough skin of his lips that spoke to weeks spent in training, in learning how to seek justice and protect others in the very way he protected her right now. She felt none of the urgency behind his kiss that she'd sensed every time she and Marc had shared a tender moment. It was as though Noel wanted to show her that things could be different— that love didn't make demands, that it wasn't self-seeking.

Wait, love? No, that couldn't be it. Not yet. Maybe not at all, not with Noel. But then his nose gently brushed against her cheek as they drew apart, and she realized she didn't want the moment to end.

How had this happened?

Hadn't she wanted it to?

His demeanor shifted as he sat back in his seat. Had he ended it? Had she? She wanted him to pull her back to him, but the sudden frown on his face shattered any illusion that he could have possibly felt the same. Her heart felt heavy as he started the vehicle, refusing to look at her.

"Noel? What's wrong?"

He cleared his throat and steered onto the road. "I shouldn't have done that."

It felt like he'd punched a hole clear through her chest. "What are you talking about? If you weren't driving, I'd pull you right back over here so you could do it again."

He sighed and glanced at her. "I'm not the right guy for you, Mina. You deserve better. Someone who can always be there for you. Who won't break any more promises."

"And you're saying you *would* break promises?" The image of Marc's smirking face sprang to mind, mocking her. Telling her that she'd never do better than him.

Noel slumped in his seat. "Not on purpose. Never on purpose. But right now, I don't even know if I have a job after this. If I do, but Crais has actually turned on us, I could very well end up working in an FBI office clear across the country. You have your bakery, and you've made a life for yourself in Newherst. I mean, even if I am able to stay at the Buffalo office, the life of an FBI special agent is highly unpredictable. I can't promise that I wouldn't break any promises."

"You'd never be unfaithful." She posed it as a statement, not a question. She felt the truth of it in their kiss, how much he cared for her. Despite his words, that kiss had revealed how much he wanted to be with her, and until that moment, she hadn't been willing to admit to herself how much she wanted to be with him, too. Life had given them this second chance, and Noel was going to throw it away? "So, you're worried you might miss out on a few date nights? Noel, I can handle unpredictable. I was in the military, remember? I'm not a fragile flower. And as long as business keeps up, I'm sure I can hire someone at the bakery to run it when I can't be there."

He shook his head, and each movement felt like another spike driven into her heart. "You deserve better. You're an amazing woman, Mina. You'll find the right man or he'll find you, and it'll be the best thing that ever happened to him." She saw him swallow, blinking too rapidly for the facade of calm displayed on the rest of his face. "I only hope he realizes it before it's too late."

The finality of his tone made her wish she could find someplace to hide by herself for a little while. She closed her eyes, trying to think of anything but the pain, which had worsened at Noel's declaration and had started to creep back through her limbs and her ribcage. At least the graze on her knee from the apartment shooting seemed like a tiny scratch compared to everything else.

They drove in silence with nothing but the hum of the SUV to keep them company. At one point, Noel turned on the radio to listen to the news, only to slam the off button the moment the news reporter started to mention the FBI alert out for "person of interest Yasmine Browder."

She blinked back the tears that stung her eyes. She'd lost everything. She truly had. The man she'd thought she loved, her brother, her apartment and many of her belongings. Noel had rejected her and she'd become a wanted woman.

If they didn't pull this off, if Noel's plan went south—the plan she hoped was currently taking up his thoughts, hence his pervasive silence—she'd be arrested, charged for assaulting an FBI agent and who knew what else. She'd go to jail. Her bakery would fail, and then she really, truly would have nothing.

She closed her eyes and pressed her fingers against her temples to ease the mounting pressure.

"I think we can do this," Noel murmured, rousing Yasmine. Her eyelids fluttered open. Had she fallen asleep? She blinked at the bright light that filtered into the vehicle, rays of morning sunlight glinting off the road signs they passed by.

She yawned, but the movement sent a fresh flood of pain to her injuries. She didn't feel as bad as the day before, but it'd still be difficult to manage without the prescription painkillers. She opened the glove box and pulled out the container of ibuprofen.

"Here." Noel picked up a bottle of water from in between their seats and handed it to her. "I got it at the last quick stop for gas. There's a plastic-wrapped muffin in a bag on the backseat if you're hungry. I grabbed it from a basket at the register while paying cash. Mine was a little stale, and you'll probably declare it a travesty of modern baking, but at this point I don't want to risk stopping until we've reached our destination. We're almost there."

She took the water and mumbled her thanks as he took one hand off the wheel and reached between the seats, still keeping his eyes on the road. His fingers hooked the plastic bag, and he dropped it in her lap.

"I could have gotten it," she said.

"You're injured and must still hurt. Otherwise you wouldn't have gone for the ibuprofen as soon as you opened your eyes. Take it, but eat so the medicine doesn't upset your stomach. Let's not add a stomachache to everything you're dealing with."

She wanted to snap at him and tell him she could handle herself—they were adults now, after all—but everything hurt too much and her head felt too fuzzy to do anything other than take the pills and eat, just like he'd suggested. She didn't want to give him the satisfaction of having been right, but what else could she do? His words to her last night echoed between her ears, pounding on the insides of her skull. They'd kissed, actually kissed. After all these years!

And he'd rejected her.

It had to be her fault. Something she'd done. Had Marc seen or felt the same thing? Was that why he'd sought love in the arms of another woman?

She couldn't seem to shake the feeling that Noel had been lying and that there really *was* something wrong with her.

"So, what's the plan?" She finished the last

bite of dry, barely palatable blueberry muffin and washed it down with the rest of the water. "Are we storming the castle?"

Noel chuckled. "More or less. I've decided that either Crais really did betray us, or he's done us a massive favor and this was part of his plan all along."

"That's a pretty big difference."

"I know. And either way, having you on the wanted list is going to get us into the Pentagon to speak with someone from the Department of Defense."

Yasmine gaped at him. "You're kidding, right? You think they're just going to let us waltz into the Pentagon with me as a federal person of interest?"

He tapped the steering wheel. "No, I don't. I think they're going to just let *me* waltz into the Pentagon, having captured a person of interest on the FBI's watch list while she was *en route* to one of the most secure buildings in North America."

There was no question about it. He'd gone crazy. "And how are you going to do that without someone shooting me?"

"I take you in as a detainee. Cuffed."

"You're going to arrest me?"

"Temporarily."

Yasmine sputtered, completely at a loss for

words. Arrest her? Bring her into the Pentagon in handcuffs? That sounded like a massive risk. "Won't they grab me and put me in a cell? Or drag me off to prison? Shouldn't we go in as equals so you can explain how I'm under your protection?"

"No. You need to understand that ninety percent of the time, guests are not allowed inside the Pentagon, and those who are go through an extensive, rigorous approval process."

"Even FBI agents?"

"Even special agents from the FBI. Not to the same extent, of course, but we can't just pop in and out, unannounced."

It felt like a vise had clamped onto her insides and begun to squeeze. "But can't you get permission? You said ninety percent of the time. What about the other ten percent?"

"That's what I'm hoping to take advantage of. And we're not going to appear without warning, because there's literally no way we'd get inside the Pentagon without advance notice. I called ahead and mentioned I'm FBI and told them that I was pursuing Yasmine Browder as she made her way to DC but that I had the situation under control. Put a call in to Captain Simcoe, too, to get any local cops off our tail. He agreed to pass information down the chain of districts to leave our vehicle alone."

She raised an eyebrow. "Pursuing me on my way to DC? I thought you were doing your best to do the opposite of that."

He winced and his eyes narrowed as he sighed. "It wasn't a lie, Yasmine, believe me. I understand why Crais refused to lie, and I agree with him. As an FBI agent, I can't lie to the people who're doing their best to protect this country, just like I am."

Yasmine wanted to push him further, to ask what he meant by that, but the road sign overhead told them that they were only about ten miles away from the Pentagon. Ten miles? Already? Her heart began to pound, and the squeezing in her stomach tightened. The muffin roiled as Noel told her the rest of the plan.

"I called ahead through the emergency line, and the person on the other end was able to verify my credentials. They said it could take up to twelve hours to approve my visitor application since I've never been there before, but I figure it'll be okay if we show up a few hours early. I'll have a person of interest in custody, after all. And since you're wanted by the FBI, and I'm FBI, they can't take you from me. Understand? You're my case. The local police aren't going to cart you off to prison.

They can't. They have no reason to unless you hijack a car or something."

Yasmine laughed, thinking of the vehicle they were driving in. "You sure Crais hasn't called this one in? Because they very well could nab me for that."

"It's still an FBI vehicle, Mina." The Suburban slowed as Noel took the next exit. "It's going to be all right. We're going to get to the bottom of this. I promise."

His words scraped at her last bit of patience. "You promise?" She couldn't keep the bitterness from her tone, feeling bad for snapping even as the words left her mouth.

He responded without hesitation. "I do. This is a promise I intend to keep, no matter what."

It was going to work. It had to work. He had to believe that Crais had looked at the bigger picture and had called in Yasmine as a wanted person for exactly this reason. Crais had said he would do what he could to help, but seeing Yasmine's picture up on the TV screen sure hadn't felt like help. Not with all those people around, eager to cash in on the posted reward.

But if Crais really had changed his mind and turned against them, at least the alert for

Yasmine would get both of them inside the Pentagon. The truth was, Noel had no idea what would happen once they passed through the front doors. Would they be detained in a visitor area until his pass got approved? He was banking on the fact that the United States government wouldn't be keen on a cuffed person of interest spending time in the visitor area of what was supposed to be a ridiculously secure military command post. Journalists, reporters and foreign heads of state moved through the visitor area. The potential for Yasmine to make a scene and cause the Department of Defense to lose face was too great to let them linger in the waiting area.

That was Noel's grand plan, anyway.

About a half mile from the parking area, Noel pulled over and withdrew a pair of handcuffs. The look on Yasmine's face brought back the tension tenfold.

"It's just for show," he said, trying to keep his voice low and calm. "I won't let anything happen to you."

"You keep saying that." She shook her head and rubbed her eyes. "If I didn't believe God was in control even now, I'd be freaking out. I'd have already leaped out of this car and been halfway back to Newherst."

"Except for the injuries, too, right?"

"Yeah. That."

He kept his mouth shut as she closed her eyes as if in prayer. With all the things that had happened to her—with everything she'd lost so far—she still trusted God to carry her through this? Why couldn't she just trust *him*?

It had been a long time since Noel cracked open his Bible, but something from those days of overhearing his mom at Bible study at Yasmine's place must have stuck with him, because a verse popped into his head. *"I will strengthen thee; yea, I will help thee."* He couldn't remember what part of the Bible it came from, but he did remember that the verse was a promise.

Was it a promise from God to the people who loved and trusted Him? That sounded right. Yasmine appeared still to love and trust God even after all she'd been through. She deserved to have a promise kept. *God, keep your promise to her,* he prayed, the first time he'd done so in a long time. Would God even listen after so many years without him speaking to Him? A quiet voice inside his heart told him that He would. *She needs someone to prove to her that she's loved. That she's worth it. And I don't think I can be that person.*

"Are we going to do this or what?" Yasmine held her wrists toward him. She looked straight at him, her gaze a challenge. He'd have to rise to meet it, because there was no way he'd let her go to jail for something she didn't do, and neither would he sit back and wait for an assassin's bullet to find its mark.

Noel wanted answers about the soldier killed in action who'd been very much alive and taken a shot at them, and he needed to know what kind of monster would be desperate enough to make multiple assassination attempts on the sister of the man who'd found them out. These people wanted to cover their tracks and tie up any loose ends, to remove any possibility of exposure, no matter how vague.

The time had come to put an end to the madness. He clicked the cuffs into place around Yasmine's wrists and met her gaze. "Are you ready?"

She nodded, and once again he saw the soldier inside her. The strong woman who'd joined the military to be with the man she'd loved. That kind of sacrifice took guts, strength and determination. If Yasmine had been willing to endure compulsory military service for the sake of love, no wonder she seemed furious with him for backing down over a little bit of distance. Over a potential broken date night or two, she'd said.

But it could be more than that. She'd risk losing her bakery. And she didn't deserve any broken date nights, none whatsoever, even if she claimed she understood the nature of his job.

But are the truth of her feelings and what she deserves to endure really my call to make if she says she can handle them?

He shook it off. Checked the cuffs to make sure they weren't too tight.

He watched as she clenched her jaw and rolled back her shoulders, a steel mask settling over her features as they approached the first parking barrier. "Let's do this."

FOURTEEN

Noel had known the parking area would be the easy part, but he couldn't help but feel a little of his tension ease as he pulled into a parking space far from prying eyes. He'd flashed his badge, and the security guard had looked him up to make sure his ID checked out, then waved them through. As they exited the vehicle and moved toward the Pentagon's visitor entrance, Noel scanned the area around them for potential threats, despite knowing that it would be nearly impossible for someone to make a surprise attack while on Pentagon grounds. Doing so would be literal suicide—though based on the recklessness of the attacks against Yasmine so far, he couldn't rule it out completely.

Noel gripped Yasmine's elbow as they walked. They reached the doors to the visitor entrance and crossed the short space of tiled floor leading to the second set of doors.

Finally they reached the metal detectors. Noel's heart pounded, nerves setting in. If they didn't make it through these detectors, they'd be back to square one, and Yasmine would find herself in even greater danger.

"Noel Black, special agent with the FBI," he said as he waved over one of the Pentagon Police, a member of one of the two special police forces trained to protect the personnel and civilians visiting and working at the Pentagon. He noted that several visiting journalists, recognizable by the way they clutched the cameras and mini recorders in their hands, had suddenly started listening in. "I called ahead about six or seven hours ago. Told them I'd gone after Yasmine Browder, wanted by the FBI, and was heading toward DC. I mentioned that if I was successful, I'd be heading to the closest government office, so—"

"Got it." The police officer waved a second man over and pulled out a walkie-talkie. The two conferred with their backs to Noel before the first officer got on the walkie-talkie to call, presumably, the visitor services desk. The Pentagon was considered one of the most secure government facilities in North America for a reason.

Yasmine gave Noel a worried look. He tried

to reassure her with a slight nod, but that only seemed to cause greater tension.

"I'm told you weren't expected here for at least another three hours," the officer finally said, holding the walkie-talkie away from his mouth.

"No, that's not what I said." Noel shook his head to emphasize the point. "I said I was about seven hours outside DC. What was I supposed to do once I had her in custody, sit in the parking lot for another three hours? Turn her over to local police? You know I can't do that."

The officer nodded and got back on the walkie-talkie. The wait during the back-and-forth between the police and whoever was on the other end felt excruciating, but Noel knew it was for the best. Better to have everyone involved believing they'd done due diligence. Finally, the officer waved him and Yasmine over to the metal detectors.

"You have to turn over your weapons," the officer said, handing Noel a plastic bin before waving Yasmine through. Noel disarmed himself and watched carefully as Yasmine stepped through the detector—of course setting it off due to her handcuffs—and then received a pat-down from a female member of the Pentagon Police who'd arrived on the scene just for that purpose. Noel returned the plastic bin to the waiting officer and stepped through.

"Are we free to head up?" Noel gestured to one of the numerous hallways branching off the area they'd entered. "I'm expected."

"Guest services," the officer said, his voice gruff. "You need your passes."

"You want me to bring a cuffed suspect in an investigation through an atrium full of journalists?"

The officer regarded Noel for a long moment, then relented. "Fine. I'll send someone for the passes, but I'll escort you wherever you need to go until you have them. Otherwise someone else will stop you, and you'll be out of here before you can say boo."

"And my sidearm?"

"Returned when you leave. Pick it up from the security office on your way out. And remember, once you have clearance, leave the visitor entrance for the visitors. You're not one of them. Use your designated entrance."

"Got it. Lead the way." Noel glanced at Yasmine to see how she was handling the situation, but her features displayed only a mask of smooth confidence...until she looked at him. Then he saw the tension behind her eyes. Trusting him was costing her a considerable amount of strength. He couldn't let her down. He cleared his throat and thought through what to say next. Where was the officer taking them, anyway? "Are you bringing us to see the chairman? Vice chairman?"

The officer paused and glanced over his shoulder. "You're here to see Chairman Furlow?"

"I put in a special request, and besides, I've detained a critical person of interest. I'm not here to speak to just anyone, Officer."

"My records show you asked to speak to someone with authority, but it didn't say exactly whom."

"It's an issue of national security. Who would you have me speak to? You think the Department of Defense wants to risk that kind of information being overheard by one of these roving journalists?"

The officer's jaw tensed. "I suppose not. This way, then." They walked down several more halls as Noel attempted to memorize the path they took. The Pentagon was a massive facility and getting lost a real possibility. If anything went wrong, he wanted to know how to get out.

Not that I expect anything to go wrong. They'd made it this far, and getting inside should've been the biggest challenge. From here on out, he figured the rest would be a comparative cakewalk.

Finally the officer stopped in front of a solid gray door with a small window at eye level. He opened the door and stepped back, holding it wide for Noel and Yasmine to enter. The room was a stark, plain office, the kind used for brief meetings with the type of people who didn't want to be seen or overheard. The setup lacked any semblance of warmth. A gray table sat in the center of the room, encircled by uncomfortable-looking metal folding chairs, and the walls had been painted cement gray. A short, plump gray-brown armchair in the furthest corner was the brightest piece. It looked like a castoff from a college dorm.

Noel nodded at the officer to acknowledge that they'd wait here. The officer spun on his heel and left, leaving the door to swing shut with a soft click. Noel had no doubt that someone else was watching the door, either in person or on a security camera, to make sure they didn't leave unaccompanied.

Yasmine sat in one of the metal chairs and plunked her cuffed hands on the table with a loud clank. "Now what? And who's the big, important guy you want us to speak to?"

Noel turned to her, placed a finger on his lips and lowered his voice to speak his next words. "We need to keep up the act in here. Keep our voices down. I don't think there are cameras or mics in a room like this, but just in case."

"Okay, fine. But shouldn't I be in the loop?" she whispered in return.

He pressed his lips together for a moment, his hands resting on his hips. "I'm hoping for one of two people. Either the chairman of the Joint Chiefs of Staff or the vice chairman."

Yasmine's eyes widened. "Oh, wow. You really think they'll let you speak to one of them?"

Noel laughed softly. "I doubt it. But the more fuss I make about getting up the chain, the more likely it is that I'll get to talk to someone closer to the top. I have a feeling they'll speak to us once I get this information in the right hands, though. It's not like the Department of Defense is going to take too kindly to learning that one of their own has been acting independently and may be responsible for several murders."

"So long as this all happens before someone arrives to cart me off." Yasmine sighed and slumped back in the metal seat. Her posture would have looked relaxed to someone who didn't know better, but Noel recognized the tension in her shoulders and the way she planted her feet, ready to spring into action at any moment. She might have spent only a short time in compulsory training, but a soldier's discipline and ability to react at a moment's notice still lived inside her, coiled and ready to strike.

They waited. Noel grew restless but remained standing, unwilling to relax until they'd seen this through. After having been on the go for hours, sitting around and waiting for someone to speak to them felt agonizing rather than restful. He wanted to be done with it so he could send Yasmine home for some much-deserved rest and peace of mind. She had to be screaming on the inside as they waited, knowing that justice for Daniel—or at least, the start of the process toward justice—was only a conversation away.

Noel checked his watch. Just over an hour had passed since they'd arrived in this room. That wasn't right. As an FBI special agent with a wanted person in custody, his request to speak with a person in authority should have been given high priority, especially considering that he'd called in his visit hours ago. Were they really going to make him wait those three extra hours? It was getting to the point that he might need to remind someone that he and Yasmine were here.

"Yasmine, I'm going to—"

A rap on the door cut his statement short. The door swung open, and a woman in a powder-blue pantsuit poked her head inside. "Special Agent Black?"

Finally. "I thought you folks had forgotten about us."

"Of course not, Agent Black." The woman offered a pleasant but tight smile. "If you wouldn't mind coming with me, however? There's someone who needs to speak with you privately." She looked pointedly at Yasmine, and Noel caught the unspoken message.

He shook his head at her request. "This woman is an FBI detainee whose life is also in danger. I'm not comfortable leaving her alone."

The woman's smile faltered, then reappeared a little stronger and a little more forced. Noel understood she was only trying to do her job and their arrival had likely inconvenienced a number of people, but what was a little inconvenience compared to Yasmine's life?

"She'll be perfectly safe here, Agent Black. She'll be watched over until you're brought back to this room. You *are* in the Pentagon, after all. I'm not sure there's anywhere safer in the whole United States."

She made an excellent point, one he couldn't disagree on. "And who will I be speaking with?"

The woman shrugged. "I know you asked to speak with Chairman Furlow or Vice Chairman Stark, but they're both currently occupied. If you'll come quickly, please? I've been told this is a matter of national security and time is of the essence."

Noel looked back at Yasmine, who stared straight ahead at the wall. She was playing her part perfectly, looking annoyed and bored and showing no trace of the anxiety that had to be roiling around inside. Slowly she turned to give him the briefest of glances. The slight dip of her chin as they locked eyes told him that she'd be okay on her own. She trusted him enough to let him go.

If only his heart could do the same with his feelings for her.

"Fine," he said, turning back to the woman in the blue pantsuit. "Lead the way."

The door closed behind Noel, leaving Yasmine alone in the plain gray room. Her heart pounded faster as the reality of being alone in a strange place settled in. She took three deep breaths, counting each one, trying to slow her heart rate. It would do no good to allow panic to creep in at a time like this.

Even if her time in Amar's military training program had been for naught thanks to Marc, she'd picked up valuable skills during her time there—many of which she'd found herself drawing on over the past few days. Had it really been less than forty-eight hours since she'd arrived home to gunshots flying through her apartment?

She stood and paced the room, checking the corners for cameras or microphones. Just because she didn't see any didn't mean they weren't there.

Lord, be with Noel as he speaks to someone about this situation, she prayed, lowering herself into the worn armchair. The painkillers she'd taken earlier in the morning had begun to wear off, and she hadn't bothered to bring any in from the car. She hadn't figured they'd be inside the Pentagon for this long. She'd need another one very soon, but she didn't want to do anything that might compromise her safety or her and Noel's position as visitors inside the building. They were so close to justice for Daniel. Putting that at risk would be foolish.

The door handle turned. A man in a black

suit entered the room, carrying a clipboard in one hand and a bottle of water in the other.

"Good afternoon, Miss... Browder, is it?"

Yasmine said nothing. He hadn't introduced himself, so why should she?

He paused as if waiting for a response, but when he didn't receive one, he set the water down on the edge of the table and then checked his clipboard.

"The FBI special agent who brought you here mentioned that you'd recently been injured in an altercation and might be in need of pain medication."

Yasmine sat up straighter at his words. Noel had told someone? It must have been on his way out of the room. She hadn't realized that he'd been paying such close attention to her medication cycle, but it made sense. Since the moment she'd thrown herself across the hood of his car and dived into the front seat, he'd had a knack for being in tune with her needs.

The man pressed the metal clip on his board and pulled off a small resealable baggie. A tiny white pill sat inside. He placed the baggie on the table and slid it toward her. "It's from our staff medical team. Nothing special, so don't get too excited."

Yasmine didn't move, but it seemed like he

planned to stand there until she said something. "Thank you."

"Of course." The man continued to stand unmoving, staring at her.

Yasmine's agitation increased. "Are you going to stay until I take it?"

"Either you take it or it leaves with me. Are you injured or not?"

She was. Of course she wanted to feel better, but something about this didn't sit well with her. Why hadn't Noel asked for the painkiller in her presence when the woman first came to take him elsewhere? She couldn't remember having mentioned her injuries or telegraphing them to anyone since they arrived, so it made sense for the request to have come from Noel. But the way this man watched her was almost...predatory. Like he'd force the pill down her throat if she didn't take it.

"What did you say your name was?" she asked, trying to buy time to think.

He smirked. "I didn't. I also have work to do. Please take the pill."

She thought about refusing. She thought about how loud she could scream if this person turned out to be unfriendly, but drawing attention to herself could put Noel at risk. They were too close to figuring out who inside the Department of Defense could have

been responsible for Daniel's death, and—
Alarm shot through Yasmine's insides. What
if this man was that person?

What if the lady was wrong and the Pentagon wasn't as safe as they'd thought? What
if the person who'd killed Daniel knew they
were here and had found them?

She looked the man in front of her square
in the eyes. No, this wasn't him. He looked
bored, like he was simply following orders
to give her the medication and make sure she
took it. He might have perfected his menac-
ing stare, but she sensed no inherent threat
from this man.

And maybe he'd only brought her a painkiller after all. If so, no harm done, and she
could attribute his brusque demeanor to the
handcuffs locked around her wrists. On the
other hand, if there was someone else waiting for her to take the pill, that someone else
would want proof she'd done so.

With her cuffed hands, she leaned toward
the table and picked up the bottle and the plastic baggie.

She opened the baggie and slipped the pill
out. It didn't look suspicious at all. In fact,
under normal circumstances, she'd assume
it to be acetaminophen.

These were far from normal circumstances.

She slid the pill onto her tongue and then uncapped the water, listening for the crack of plastic as she twisted the top. When it came, she felt mild relief that no one had tampered with the water. But if she took a drink, the water would dissolve some of the pill, even if she didn't swallow.

Think, Yasmine, think. In the army, she'd learned many tactics for avoiding manipulation and resisting coercion. Stealth techniques were a standard part of the curriculum, for which she'd never been more grateful during these past few days.

She needed to draw on that again.

She lifted the bottle to her lips and turned her face away from the watching man. With her right cheek facing the back of the armchair, she positioned the mouth of the bottle at the far corner of her lips to create an illusion of taking a drink. She tilted the bottle back, pretending to tip the water into her mouth. Instead, a small amount hit the back of the armchair as she flipped the pill underneath her tongue and swallowed air.

She lowered the bottle and turned around to see a look of satisfaction on the waiting man's face. He took in the contents of the bottle— saw it was no longer full—and nodded.

"Thanks," she said, to continue the facade.

"You're welcome. Hang tight. This will all be taken care of soon." He turned and left, his words hanging with an ominous finality.

Yasmine leaned back in the armchair, feeling the wet spot press against her back and soak part of her shirt. Good thing she'd been sitting here instead of in one of those metal chairs—inconspicuously pouring water down a sleeve or shirt was far more difficult and prone to error. She dislodged the pill from under her tongue and spit it into her hands, then twisted slightly to shove it between the chair cushion and its base.

She'd been left alone, but for how long? If the little white pill really had been a normal painkiller, she expected that the next person she'd see would be Noel. But if not?

Better safe than sorry.

Yasmine inhaled, taking deep breaths in and out. One at a time. Slow and steady, calming her pulse. With each breath, she deepened her focus inward on the beat of her heart, and pretended to die.

FIFTEEN

Yasmine's pulse slowed with each breath. She'd always been good at pretending to be asleep, even as a child—she'd found no end of delight in playing practical jokes on Daniel when they were younger, "waking up" when he least expected it and turning his own pranks back on him. One time he'd come home with a tiny frog he'd found at the park after a rainstorm and placed it on her pillow while she slept, intending to frighten her. He'd had no way of knowing that she'd actually woken up the moment he entered her room and was ready for him. She'd waited until he put the poor frog down, his face right in front of hers as he concentrated on keeping the frog in place until she woke, and then popped open her eyes with a loud "Ribbit!"

Daniel had shrieked and tumbled backward as she sat up, scooping the little frog into her hands while laughing at her brother's shocked expression.

"You should have seen your face!" she'd said, laughing so hard she gasped for breath.

"You were supposed to be asleep," he'd grumbled, his cheeks growing scarlet. Yasmine had continued to laugh for a solid five minutes before climbing out of bed to run outside and let the little frog go free.

She drew on that childhood experience, complemented with her survival training from the Amaran military, to send herself into a near trancelike state that mimicked sleep. She allowed her head to loll forward at an uncomfortable angle, the same way it might hang if she'd suddenly fallen unconscious in the chair.

Footsteps sounded outside the door. Her body tensed in anticipation, but she coaxed it back into relaxation as the door handle turned. This was it, the moment of truth. Had Noel sent the painkillers or was she truly not safe even deep inside the Pentagon?

Someone entered the room in silence. No, two people. There were too many taps against the floor for one person.

"That's her," said a quiet voice. "I watched her take it."

The response from the second person was

muffled. He or she was likely standing with his or her back to Yasmine.

"You need me to check?" asked the first person.

Yasmine struggled to maintain composure as footsteps came toward her. Rough fingers pressed against the side of her neck.

"Pulse is slow," said the first voice. Definitely the man who'd brought her the pill. She took another deep breath and exhaled. "I can barely feel it. Can't be much longer."

"Good," said the muffled voice. The fingers left her neck and she heard the first man cross the floor, back toward the door. "It's about time for…to end."

Yasmine almost stiffened. The muffled speaker had lowered his voice further—it was definitely a man who spoke—and she could hardly make out his next words.

"See… Crais…" he said. "He's here, so… take care of…" Yasmine strained to hear more, but they'd opened the door and stepped out before they'd finished speaking.

Crais. Noel's FBI mentor was in the building? He'd come to the Pentagon, too?

As soon as the door clicked back into place, Yasmine opened her eyes and sat up, her neck aching from hanging at an awkward angle for so long. She rubbed the sore muscles as she crossed the room to the door, a gesture made all the more uncomfortable by the handcuffs that still connected her wrists together. She'd have to do something about that, but how? She had no key, no sharp implement...and then her eyes landed on the clipboard left behind on the table. The pill guy must have left it in the room after his visit. She rushed back to the table, holding her breath.

There it was: a paperclip, slid onto the edge of several papers, metallic and shining like a beacon of hope. With deft fingers, Yasmine snatched up the clip, unbent it and used the straightened length to unlock the cuffs from her wrists. She slid the metal constraints off and tucked them in her back pocket. Then, freed and driven by a need to find Noel before Crais did, she pressed her ear against the door. Hearing no one, she gripped the door handle and turned it. She waited for the tell-tale click of the door unlocking and sent a quick prayer of thanks to the Almighty that the men who'd come to check on her hadn't bothered to lock the door. After all, why lock the door on a dead woman?

She glanced both directions down the hall-way and saw no one, but she had a feeling she wouldn't be left alone for long. She also remembered how many cameras she'd seen on their way to this room—it was only a matter of time before someone glanced at the correct camera display and saw a strange woman wandering the halls of the Pentagon without an ID badge.

She needed to find Noel before the wrong someone else did. But how? Yasmine scooted to the end of the hallway and peeked around the corner. Her heart sank. Cubicles. The people working there seemed occupied with their work, but she couldn't guarantee that no one would look up and wonder what she was doing there.

Her mind raced. She had two critical tasks: to find Noel and to figure out where Crais was before he found them first, just in case. A million different ways to solve each problem independently raced through her mind, but nothing that would ensure she succeeded at both without getting herself arrested a second time. And whoever had tried to kill her just now would certainly find out and try again. She had no doubt they wouldn't fail given a second chance behind government walls. Only one possibility came to mind that might work, but it was crazy. There was no way it could succeed.

"Fear thou not; for I am with thee: be not dismayed." A turn of phrase from her moth-

er's favorite Bible verse popped into her head. Her mother had that verse written out and posted in at least three places in their house when growing up, but the frequency of seeing it had meant that Yasmine's eyes soon glossed over the words, easily forgotten and unnoticed in the familiarity.

She'd never really thought about what it meant until now. Her options were running short, and time was of the essence. Did that mean this one crazy idea was the right one? If she didn't try, someone was bound to come along the hallway behind her at any moment and discover that Yasmine Browder hadn't died in that room like they'd planned.

Fear thou not. She shook her head and bounced on her heels several times. This was it. Everything could end right here, right now, but she had to try.

Yasmine plastered a goofy smile on her face and forced a bubbly laugh, turning the corner out of the hallway and walking toward the closest cubicle. She scanned the space quickly as she approached, looking for something with the employee's name on it. There it was, a sign facing out with the woman's name and credentials. Janie Sherwood, Public Relations. *Perfect.*

"Hey, Janie. Have any FBI agents come

through here recently? I need to meet up with Crais and Black, but got detained by internal affairs. No one has bothered to let me know which room either of them headed off to."

None of what she'd said was not true. Yasmine understood and respected what Noel had said earlier—lying to these people was neither appropriate nor fair. They were only trying to do their jobs to keep the country safe, but at the same time, she and Noel didn't know whom they could or couldn't trust. Never had this been more apparent than moments ago in that stark little room.

Muscles in Janie's face twitched and then relaxed at the mention of Crais's name. "Special Agent John Crais? I've met him only a few times, but he thinks he's something else, doesn't he?"

Yasmine grinned and shrugged. "Who can even understand what goes through that man's head? I'm late for the meeting now. It's going to be awkward when I walk in the room, that's for certain."

Janie hesitated, looking Yasmine up and down. "You okay? You look like you've been through the wringer."

"You know what it's like. One day you wake up for an eight-hour shift and the next thing you know, two days have gone by and you've eaten nothing but a stale muffin and you're almost wishing you'd been shipped out, because at least then you'd have had a chance to get some sleep on the red-eye flight you'd inevitably be on because of how much cheaper it is."

Janie laughed but shook her head. "Sorry, but I'm not sure where external agency meetings are being held today. Probably in the usual rooms."

"Got it." Yasmine waved her thanks, masking her disappointment that she hadn't gotten all the information she wanted—but if Janie had seen Crais a few times, that meant he'd passed this way on his visits. She had to be close. Otherwise he and Janie would never have crossed paths multiple times, right? Yasmine massaged her wrists and offered up a grateful smile. "Thanks, appreciate it."

She'd gone only five steps before she heard Janie's voice behind her. "Hey, excuse me?"

Yasmine kept walking, pretending she couldn't hear.

"Excuse me? Ma'am? Agent?" Janie's voice grew louder. "You've lost your badge!"

Yasmine swallowed the sudden lump in her throat, quickened her steps and disappeared around the corner, Janie's shouts quieting behind her. As soon as she was back out of sight of the cubicles, Yasmine raced down the hall, moving away from the room where she'd been detained. She heard no footsteps following her, but she kept up the pace just in case Janie alerted someone to the direction Yasmine had traveled. Yasmine would have to move fast if she wanted to avoid detection.

She glanced in each room as she passed, listening carefully for familiar voices, movement or any indication that Crais or Noel might be behind one of the doors. Very few of the rooms had drawn shades over the windows, which made her think—if Crais was in one of these rooms, and if he in fact had double-crossed them and was part of a big conspiracy at the Department of Defense, wouldn't he be the one sitting behind a drawn shade?

She allowed herself a little smile at the thought. She'd find Crais, and soon. But that wasn't her only problem. Where was Noel? And what would happen if he went back to the room where he'd left her, only to find that she'd disappeared?

Noel followed the woman leading the way for what seemed like ages. They walked down one hallway and up another, then made a left turn and a right turn and another right turn. After at least fifteen minutes of walking, Noel realized that all the doors they were passing looked familiar.

"Excuse me?" He tapped his guide on the shoulder.

"Hmm?" She looked back at him with disinterest.

"Why are you taking me in circles?"

Her eyebrows rose, giving away the truth. "I'm not."

"Yes, you are. Are you trying to confuse me? Because I have an excellent sense of direction."

Her expression darkened, and she turned back around, continuing to walk. Noel grunted in frustration. What else could he do but follow? The woman had obviously been instructed to kill time and thought she could do it by confusing him in the network of hallways. She clearly hadn't counted on escorting a man fresh out of Quantico, whose skills of observation had been put to the test day in and day out for the past twenty weeks.

Finally she stopped in front of a door that looked like all the others, except the shade was drawn.

"Here," she said, her pleasant expression long gone. "General Stark will be with you shortly."

So she'd been trying to stall on orders from

the vice chairman himself? He'd have been more annoyed if he wasn't so impressed that General Stark had actually agreed to speak with him. "Trying to make sure I don't get up to any trouble on my own?"

She frowned. "Something like that." The woman twisted the handle, pushed the door open and stepped aside. "Wait here for the general, please."

Noel resisted the urge to roll his eyes and stepped inside. The room was dark, the back half cloaked in shadow. Where was the light switch? He felt along the wall as the woman closed the door behind him, leaving him in the dark. He felt like he was in the dark metaphorically speaking, too. Talking to one of the higher-ups of the Department of Defense should bring some relief, but he couldn't imagine they'd react kindly when he accused one of their own. Not at first, anyway. He'd have to be diplomatic about the conversation and find a way for the FBI alert to be removed from Yasmine. At least Yasmine was safe inside the Pentagon, though he still didn't like the idea of leaving her on her own. She'd need her next dose of painkillers soon, and she probably hadn't thought to bring any inside from the vehicle when they'd arrived. He considered running back down the hall to catch the woman and ask her to take some painkillers to Yasmine, but movement at the back of the room froze his hand on the door handle.

His fingers crept up the side of the wall, searching for the light switch. He tensed, turning and bringing his right hand up in a defensive pose. And then he flicked on the lights.

John Crais stood at the back of the room, palms raised in surrender. "Don't yell, Black. I'm here to help you, just like I promised. Tami, the woman who escorted you here, thinks she left you in an empty room after making sure you were all turned around. But I trust you know where you are?"

Noel's jaw tensed and he ground his teeth. How was Crais here? And why? "Trust? You put Yasmine on the FBI wanted list. You'd better give me one good reason why I should trust *you*."

Crais shrugged. "It got you inside the Pentagon, didn't it?"

So Crais had known it would work all along. Maybe he *was* on their side. "Why are you waiting in here in the dark?"

It was Crais's turn to look upset. "I came here because somebody thinks they can get to me. I told you yesterday about my orders, but the pressure mounted after I came to. That Browder woman sure packs a wallop."

Noel nearly snorted. "Tell me about it."

Crais moved closer, lowering his voice. "After issuing the alert, I hopped the first flight here. It took some maneuvering, but I've been waiting here for your arrival. I was able to learn that this is where General Stark will speak with you about the Department of Defense account you discovered. I assume you have more information now? Aside from what we discussed at the safe house?"

"Yes," Noel said, trying to keep up. Crais needed to get up to speed, too, so Noel filled him in on what they'd learned from Shaun's digging. "But why is General Stark going to speak to me?"

Why would the vice chairman of the Joint Chiefs of Staff actually consent to speak to him? The best he'd hoped for was one of the man's advisors. A classic negotiation technique was to ask for more than one wanted, expecting to receive less. But for the general to deign to speak with someone like Noel, barely even out of the FBI Academy...

"Think about it," Crais said. "You called in this information last night, right?"

Noel nodded. "I did."

"It would have been passed up the chain,

and it should have been stopped and cut down by the person who was responsible for the secret account. That would have provided a clue where along the chain of command things fell apart. But it didn't. It went all the way to the top, Black. The news stopped with General Stark alone, who has personally agreed to speak with you."

Noel gaped at Crais as the situation became clearer. The funds. The influence. The power. The incredible reach and ability to recruit soldiers to be officially reported killed in action, then bringing them back to life with new identities. The amount of money and organizational skills it would take to manage an operation like that and the experience it would take to keep it quiet—permanently. The manpower required to tie up any potential loose ends, no matter how slight.

"It's General Stark," Noel murmured. "He's behind this. He's behind everything."

Crais nodded. "I've done some poking around on my own since I arrived, and all signs point to Stark. This goes higher than I could have foreseen."

"So, how do we stop him?"

"We don't," Crais said, his voice taking on a tinge of sadness. "The general is in the Press Briefing Room for the daily broadcast right now, but it won't be long before he reaches this room. If you try to run, the idea is that you'll be too turned around to know where to go."

"And I won't get out of the meeting alive, anyway." Noel squeezed his hands into fists. If the general found him here, he'd be able to kill Noel—and probably Crais—and get away with it without anyone blinking. He could claim almost anything as the vice chairman of the Joint Chiefs of Staff and the government would back him, especially with the amount of money and reach he'd accumulated. Noel's stomach sank in despair, the inevitability of failure settling in. "How can we stop this? I'm a brand-new agent, Crais. I have no pull or influence, and if you dare to make this kind of accusation—"

"I'll lose my job, and the next person who takes over for me will inevitably be in the general's pocket. There are few people higher up, and with more influence in the government than Stark, especially in post-9/11 America." Crais dropped his hands to his hips and stared at the floor, his head shaking as if in disbelief at his next words. "The way I see it, we convince either Chairman Furlow or the POTUS himself."

"Or everyone," said a woman's voice.

Noel whirled around as Crais looked up. Yasmine stood in the doorway. Noel's heart leaped and then plummeted at the look on her face—scared but determined. "How did you find me? What are you doing in here? How… how did you leave the holding room?"

"Long story. Short version is I pressed my ear against every door with a drawn shade in this hallway until I heard familiar voices." Yasmine grimaced and tilted her chin at Crais. "We're trusting him? He didn't betray us?"

"I didn't." Crais raised his palms toward them. "I've read Noel's records from the Academy. I know how he thinks. It's why I accepted him to the Buffalo FBI branch and agreed to be his mentor."

"You knew we'd use the FBI alert as a way inside," Yasmine said. Noel resisted a strong urge to reach out and pull her into an embrace, but the look on her face told him that she hadn't made her way to this room for a social visit. "I heard some of what you were talking about through the door before I came in, but you need to know that Stark isn't acting independently. He has other people working here at the Pentagon. At least, that's my assumption about the people who just tried to kill me."

"What?" Noel stepped toward her, fury rising. "How?"

"With a painkiller that wasn't a painkiller. Two men came to check my pulse, but I managed to throw them off and make my way here. We can discuss the details later, but right now, I want to know—why did the men who tried to kill me mention Crais?"

Noel whirled around to Crais. "Explain."

"Those must be the guys who tried to recruit me into the scheme, probably working for Stark. I suspect they're the ones who communicated Stark's orders to the FBI. I suggested we meet in DC and talk, since I planned to fly here as soon as I set up the alert on Miss Browder, but I took off from our meeting once I'd confirmed my information. Either they think I'm on a very long lunch break in the staff cafeteria or they've realized I've declined their offer. Either way, I'm as much a target as you are."

"Breaking up their party is going to be mighty difficult," Noel muttered. "What did you mean when you said we could convince everyone?" He looked at Yasmine, who now leaned against the wall next to the door. Dark circles of exhaustion ringed her eyes, and the natural bronze of her complexion had turned ruddy from the lack of sleep and proper nutrition, but part of him thought she'd never looked more beautiful. Here was a woman who'd run from bullets and been willing to joke about it afterward, who'd lost so much and yet refused to give up or give in. Even her faith still held strong.

If they made it through this, he would never let her go again. Never. No matter how difficult it might be to stay together, he couldn't deny the truth. He loved her, deeply and fully, and even if he ended up stationed in Los Angeles or Austin or anywhere at all, he would fly across the country every morning and every night if it meant spending even one hour with her.

Ten years they'd been apart. From this moment on, he knew that even ten minutes away from her would make his heart ache.

"Yasmine—" His voice lowered to a whisper as she met his eyes. She shook her head, stopping his words.

"The Press Briefing Room," she said. "We don't have much time."

Noel shoved his emotions aside and focused on words. "Stark is there right now."

"Actually," Crais said, tapping his watch, "he's done. He's on his way here, so you'd better move out. The Press Briefing Room will be empty, but why go there?"

Yasmine pulled back the shade that covered the door's small window and looked both ways. "I'll explain on the way. Do either of you know how to get there?"

Crais spoke up. "Go straight down the hall and turn right. It'll take you there the long way, but if Stark is headed to this room, you can't risk running into him. Once you've turned right, take another left and you'll circumvent the short route. Once you see Press Briefing Room listed on the directional placards at the entrance of each hallway, follow those."

Noel stepped toward Yasmine as she turned the handle, but laid his hand on her shoulder as he looked back at Crais. His mentor hadn't moved. "You're not coming?"

Crais shook his head. "I'll stall him here as long as I can."

"You'll put your own life at risk."

"I'm doing my job, Black. And I'll ask you to do the same. Now, go."

With a nod at his mentor, he turned back to Yasmine. "You have a plan?"

"I do." She began to open the door but seemed to think better of it. Then, so quickly that he'd barely realized it had happened until it was over, she whirled around and planted a nimble kiss on his lips.

Then she opened the door and slipped out, and he followed. He wanted to believe that the kiss was her way of saying she loved him, too.

There was only one way to find out: they had to stop the people after Yasmine and escape the facility alive. But with someone like General Stark possibly behind the violent attacks and the mysterious banking accounts, Noel was becoming increasingly unsure of anything at all.

SIXTEEN

Yasmine followed Crais's directions, sensing that Noel kept pace behind her. She checked each corner before proceeding, but even so they had to duck into an alcove more than once as employees passed by. Strangely, no one seemed to be in a hurry, and no alerts sounded.

"Why hasn't anyone come after us?" Yasmine mumbled as they followed the third sign they'd seen for the Press Briefing Room.

"Raising an alarm might cause too many people to ask questions," Noel said. "Especially with FBI agents on the premises. I have no doubt that some of the general's lackeys are hunting us down, though, especially knowing two of them already tried to take you out of the picture. Again. The longer we're in these hallways, the more likely it is they'll find us."

As if on cue, a set of doors loomed at the end of the next hall. A plaque beside the doors indicated that they'd reached the Pentagon Press Briefing Room, while an inconspicuous door to the left, a few yards down, was identifiable by a small sign that read Technical Room.

"That's what we need," Yasmine said, waving Noel forward. The hallway was empty, and Yasmine held her breath as she gripped the handle of the tech room door. It turned without resistance, and they both slipped inside.

The broadcast booth sat empty of personnel, but the equipment remained full of life. Banks of computers, soundboards and screens were set up in a long line facing a massive glass window. Through the window, the tech team could monitor the actual Press Briefing Room, which was set up with a podium, a Department of Defense backdrop and rows of chairs lined up from the front to the back of the room.

A surge of hope at finding everything still fired up sent Yasmine rushing across the room to the computer bank. "If they've just finished, the tech team must be on break after the morning broadcast. This is even better than I'd hoped. We don't have to talk anyone into helping us."

Noel joined her, staring at the equipment

as though it might bite him. "You said you want to—what—broadcast the information?"

Yasmine waved her hand at Noel. "Phone." He handed it to her as she hunted for a cable. Finding it, she plugged the phone into the computer tower and slipped into a chair. "Exactly. Look at the screen over there." She pointed at a monitor mounted in the upper corner of the room.

Noel squinted at it. "There's another broadcast in two hours about, uh, some defense policy. Is this normal? I knew the Pentagon did live broadcasts, but I didn't realize they were so regular."

Yasmine shrugged, her fingers flying over the keyboard. She opened her phone's storage on the monitor and began to transfer the files they'd received from Shaun the day before. "I know only because of Daniel. He once told me about this because he was so excited to be a part of a facility contracted by the Department of Defense. He read the entire Department website and liked to watch the broadcasts on his days off. He loved hearing about how his work was making a difference in the lives of people, and he took pride in knowing that he was a link in the chain that kept this country safe and secure."

Her voice hitched as her emotions threatened to take over, but suddenly Noel's hands were on her shoulders, reassuring her. His presence reminded her that she wasn't alone in this—neither the moment nor her grief.

"We're going to end this, Mina. Right now." He whispered the words in her ear, gentle and yet full of strength. She couldn't help but shiver. Why had she kissed him before they'd left the room to head here? She wanted to tell herself that it was a fluke, an anxious gesture in the moment done out of panic and thankfulness that she'd found him, but she knew better than that.

When she'd seen Noel, her heart had flipped upside down, and it had been all she could do not to fall into his arms. How had she come to be so reliant on him, so willing to depend on him, despite so many years apart?

Because we're meant to be together, came a still, small voice inside. *Because you love him, even after all this time.*

He treated her as an equal and respected her need not to sit back and wait for things to happen. He knew she could take care of herself, and these past few days had shown that they worked together well as a team in dire circumstances. Would they be able to work together just as well without bullets flying or bad guys chasing them?

She didn't know, but sitting there with Noel's hands on her shoulders—knowing that he had complete confidence in her plan—made her anxious to try. She wanted to tell him, to turn around and let him know that she didn't care if she had to sell the bakery in Newherst. She'd start another one somewhere else. They could make it work, if only he was willing to give them a chance.

But they needed to make it through this day first. Telling him now would be a distraction, and they were going to require every ounce of focus for the next few minutes.

She loaded the last file onto the computer and yanked the cable out of her phone. "Noel, hit that switch over there." She pointed to the soundboard a few feet away, then returned her attention to the screen while she loaded up the broadcasting program that had been up on the screen when they'd stepped into the room.

Her heart squeezed as she navigated the program. It was, without a doubt, because of Marc that she interacted with the program with ease. He'd been an information technology specialist for a reason, and she hadn't been able to help but absorb some of his ability and knowledge during their years together.

For the first time since she'd boarded the airplane to return to the United States, she felt grateful for her relationship with Marc while it had lasted. It hadn't been for nothing. Without those years, however much she'd felt they'd been wasted up until this moment, she wouldn't have known that the button she was about to click on the broadcast program's screen would be the thing that might save their lives and finally, *finally* bring justice for Daniel.

She clicked the button and stood. "Let's get inside that room."

Noel nodded, trusting her without question, and headed to the inside door that connected both rooms. He paused as she came up behind him.

"What is it? Let's go. The information is going live."

"I know. I just— Before we go in there, I need to say something. I'm sorry for pushing you away in the car last night. I thought I knew what was best for you and for me, but—"

"You were wrong?" The tension around Yasmine's insides began to ease. "I've been wrong, too. I didn't see—I didn't *want* to see—what's been in front of me all this time. I don't know why this is happening, and I wish that seeing you again had been under better circumstances."

"But God's reasons aren't our reasons." He smiled as Yasmine's eyes widened in surprise. Had she heard him correctly? "I know, I know. I'm learning. Your faith and strength makes me feel strong, Mina, and I want the assurance you have as you face obstacles head-on. I know it's my own fault for pushing God away, but you've shown me that having faith doesn't mean giving in. It makes you stronger, more courageous. I love you for it, and I want that, too."

The air rushed from Yasmine's lungs as she processed his words. "You...what?"

He smiled, gentle and sweet and tinged with the anxiety of the moment. "I love you. And when we get through this, I'm going to show you how much. We can make it work. I know we can. But for now?" He leaned forward and planted a kiss on her lips, as rushed and yet full of hope as the one she'd given him only minutes before.

She parted her lips to speak, searching for the right words to respond, but he shook his head and pulled the door open a crack.

"Uh-uh. Later. The information is going live, remember?" He winked and stepped through the door as Yasmine forced herself to breathe again. She followed him through, her heart light and surging with joy. They

walked to the front of the room, heading toward the podium where she would expose the
general's schemes to the whole world, and—

A muffled bang split the room. In front of
her, Noel faltered, stumbled and gripped the
podium, confusion and sudden fear rippling
across his face. Had anyone else heard that?
Of course not, Yasmine realized—this was
a room used for official broadcasts and re-
cordings, and would most definitely be sound-
proofed from the rest of the building's noise.

Noel's eyes met hers, and she saw the agony
of defeat the moment before her gaze was
drawn to the drip of red against the room's
gray carpet. Noel clutched at his leg, grimacing.

General Stark stood at the Pentagon Press
Briefing Room door. Special Agent John Crais
stood with him, Stark's gun now pressed into
his side.

"Hello, Special Agent Black. Miss Browder.
I think it's about time we met, don't you?"

"General Stark." At his side, Yasmine hissed
the name through clenched teeth. Noel wanted
to reach out and offer comfort, but it was all
he could do to cling to the podium and remain
upright. The shot had hit his upper leg, immediately dredging up old fears and doubt. What

if it took years to heal again? What if this shot had just taken away everything he'd worked so hard for...and what if he couldn't protect Yasmine from whatever happened next? He prayed silently that the wound was superficial enough to allow him to act if he had the chance. *I refuse to be terrified or discouraged, Lord*, he prayed. *I know You're with Yasmine, and I believe You're with me, too.*

"Either of you decide to play the hero, and the next one goes through his stomach." General Stark shoved Crais away from him. Crais stumbled forward, coming to a stop between Stark and Yasmine. Stark waved his gun as he spoke as if he didn't have a care in the world. "Or your mentor's skull, Agent Black. It'll be far more difficult to explain away than what happened to Miss Browder's brother, but I feel that there's a good story to be concocted here about a new agent being unable to handle the pressures of the Bureau. Or something about how you were both involved in a plot against the United States, blah blah, national security. You know the buzzwords as well as I do."

He did. And Noel had no doubt that General Stark had the connections and the finances to cover this up or explain it away without question, just as he'd done so far. As vice chairman of the Joint Chiefs of Staff, who could stand against his word? And if anyone tried to oppose him, he'd simply have them killed. Just like he'd admitted doing to Daniel.

The man was a murderer, plain and simple.

Noel's hope faded as their options seemed to drain away, but when he glanced at Yasmine, he nearly lost his grip on the podium. She appeared not only determined but also... assured. The hard mask on her face exuded a confidence that he had trouble finding inside himself. Where was that coming from?

Did it matter? He loved her all the more for it.

"So you admit you had my brother killed," she said, almost shouting her words. Why was she speaking so loud? They were the only ones in the room.

Or were they?

"An unavoidable casualty, Miss Browder," Stark said, stepping forward. He lowered his gun and held it at his side as though he didn't even expect resistance. The man was fearless. "But your brother was snooping around in things that were none of his business."

"None of his business? I think the safety of American soldiers is everyone's business, especially for someone like Daniel, who believed in the work he did at the inspection facility—work you deliberately sabotaged for your own financial gain. Falsified inspection reports put good soldiers at risk, General, and you had my brother murdered for trying to keep this country safe. Just like *you're* supposed to be doing. How can you live with yourself?"

Noel watched for surprise or shock to flit across the general's face—something, anything, that said they had him backed into a corner. Instead, General Stark laughed.

"Financial gain?" He laughed again, his shoulders shaking with cruel mirth. "You stupid, shortsighted fools. Have you not been paying attention at all?" He held up his hand and gestured with two fingers. Suddenly five men in black armor poured out from behind the Department of Defense backdrop and fell into formation around the room, surrounding them.

"Back entrance," Noel muttered, feeling like one of the fools Stark accused them of being. "There's a prep room behind the backdrop. Of course. I should have known."

"Yes, you should have. I can get anyone into anywhere, even the most secure building in the country. Haven't you figured that out by now?" General Stark gave Noel a bemused look. "And my dear Miss Browder, financial gain was never my aim. Yes, I ordered the facility to falsify the inspection reports, but the only person getting financial kickbacks was Anthony Clarke, and I imagine he used some of that to ensure his employees remained cooperative. You'd be surprised how a little boost in one's bank account can encourage a person to cooperate without question."

Noel's rage increased as the general spoke. Yasmine was right—this man was responsible for keeping the country safe, and yet he'd deliberately put his own men, the country's own protectors, at unnecessary risk. "Your corruption is despicable, *sir*." Noel resisted the sudden urge to spit at the man's feet. "You've betrayed everything this country stands for, everything this facility we stand inside of works to protect."

"That's where you're wrong." Stark took several quick steps toward Noel, his anger finally surfacing. "I've always served my country, and I would do anything necessary to protect its interests. There is no corruption here, no personal gain."

"Then where is the money going?" Yasmine shouted at him, her entire body leaning forward as if she was prepared to attack at any moment. "Who does the mystery account belong to?" General Stark faltered. He blinked, then peered at Yasmine as though seeing her for the first time. "That's right. We know all about the money trails. Emails, financial reports, everything. We have proof of your corruption. We can even show you. How do you answer for that?"

"Oh, you *will* show me. I'm afraid that's the sort of information that I've trained my black ops team to dispose of, regardless of the source. Digital, human, it doesn't matter. That's how I keep America safe, Miss Browder. My team is under my leadership alone, not beholden to the restrictive laws of the land, because our enemies don't play by the same rules we do."

Like a candle lit in a dark room, General Stark's words illuminated everything. The attacks on Yasmine. How their attackers knew Noel was FBI and understood how to try to stop him from protecting her. The constant, unrelenting pursuit of Yasmine, whose brother might have told her what he'd found out about the inspection facility—and why the soldier who'd shot at Yasmine in the diner would be willing to take his own life rather than give up even one word of information. Stark had developed an obedient, lethal and highly illegal black ops team made up of soldiers supposedly killed in action that had no true oversight—because he *was* the oversight.

Money could accomplish almost anything, including getting a team of deadly soldiers into the Pentagon under the general's orders, just like it convinced an inspection facility operator to lie on his inspection reports and get those reports passed through multiple levels of gatekeepers at the Department of Defense.

The general's influence and reach, his solitary control of massive finances and his position of power in the government had enabled him to develop a covert, unregulated team that operated under the radar.

General Stark's face split in a slow, wide grin. "I can see that you understand now. And of course, that means you'll also understand why I can't allow you to leave this room. My men will take care of the mess and no one will ever be the wiser. I assure you, Special Agents, Miss Browder, that this country will be a better place thanks to your sacrifice. We can't have you exposing this operation and bringing something so pedestrian as legality into this, you realize. Boys? On my signal."

He raised his hand, fingers pointed upward. The five black-clad operatives that surrounded them dropped into a firing stance and aimed their weapons.

Noel couldn't act. The pain in his leg had

worsened, and there were too many operatives around the room for Crais and Yasmine
to take on.

This was it. The end for all of them. There
was no escaping this time, despite everything
they'd done—despite everything he'd done to
keep Yasmine safe.

I'm sorry, he wanted to say, but Yasmine
wasn't looking at him. Did she blame him
for this? He'd thought they felt the same way
about each other, and if his life had to end
right here and right now, he would do whatever he could to spare her pain.

He tensed his muscles, ready to leap from
the podium and cover her with his body.
Maybe God would be merciful and he could
shield her from the end. Maybe Stark would
accept his and Crais's deaths and let her go.
Maybe—

"Ready," said Stark.

It would never work. Noel knew that deep
inside. But if they were going to die, he
wanted the end to come with her name on
his lips.

"Aim," said Stark.

"Yasmine," Noel whispered, hoping she
would turn and look at him. But she didn't.
He spoke to her anyway. "I love you."

Stark's smile grew wider.

SEVENTEEN

"Wait!" Yasmine shouted.

Stark's smile faltered. His fingers shook with tension as they pointed upward, only a blink away from slicing through the air with the order that would end the lives of three people inside the room. In that moment of hesitation, when she knew without a doubt that the man was not bluffing, she struck.

"Wave to the camera, General Stark." She raised her arm and pointed to the blinking red light at the upper back corner of the room.

Stark's smile vanished completely. "Hold your fire," he growled. His gaze flicked up at where she pointed. "What...?"

"It's been a fascinating broadcast, General," she said, trying to keep the tremor from her voice. Adrenaline surged through her body, giving her another momentary respite from the pain of the past few days. She didn't know for sure if the broadcast had worked or if the files had appeared on-screen the way she'd tried to program into the system during the few minutes they'd had in the tech room. She prayed that she'd gotten it right, and that would have to do.

"It's being broadcast live," Noel said beside her, his voice increasing in strength and tinged with wonder. "Throughout the Pentagon. And on the Department of Defense website, thanks to the Department's very forward-thinking policy of streaming your daily briefing sessions."

He glanced at Yasmine, and her heart soared. "Now the whole country knows what you've been doing," she said.

General Stark's complexion paled and then reddened in a burst of anger. "What have you *done*?" With a shout, he raised his gun and aimed at Yasmine. Time seemed to slow down as she saw his finger itch along the trigger, tensing—

And then the doors to the Press Briefing Room flew open as swarms of heavily armed soldiers, agents and Pentagon Police poured into the room to disarm Stark and his operatives.

It was over, and Stark knew it. Fighting back would end in nothing but bloodshed on both sides, and by surrendering, he could at least try to defend himself in military court. He'd lose, Yasmine knew, but the man was too proud to admit defeat before he'd exhausted all his options.

And in that moment, as the general lifted his face to look at her, she realized he had one option left that she hadn't considered. A defiant echo of a smile crossed his face. His jaw twitched.

"No!" Yasmine shouted and Noel, spurred to action and likely realizing what the general was about to do in the same moment she did, launched himself toward the vice chairman.

Noel shoved his fingers inside the general's mouth and yanked as the man gagged. Noel's hand slid out holding a small white capsule.

"Tell your men to stand down or I promise that you'll be tried for the murder of each and every one of them." Noel handed the cyanide capsule to Crais, who tucked it away for safekeeping. "You know the system. You'll get a fair trial in military court, but if even one of your operatives ends his life today while in custody, you can kiss your chances of ever seeing the sun again goodbye. Order your men to remove their capsules."

Stark's features hardened. He'd thought he had one more round in the chamber, and they'd blocked it.

"We won't ask again," said Crais. "Remember, this is all being broadcast around the world. You could use whatever miniscule goodwill this will give you."

"Hah! You think you've won? You may have those of us in this room, but my men have a mission and they will carry it out. Your pathetic attempts haven't stopped a thing."

"Watch us."

Stark glared at Crais, but the man didn't budge. After several tense moments, Stark looked at the nearest black-clad operative, who knelt on the floor with his hands over his head. With nothing but a nod from Stark, the operative opened his mouth. The rest followed suit. Crais circled the room, pulling the cyanide capsules from their mouths, ensuring none could choose death over answering for their crimes.

Yasmine stared after Stark and the operatives as the Pentagon Police led them away. "I think it's over. We did it."

A hand landed on her shoulder, and she flinched in surprise—but seeing Noel's face only inches from hers brought her back to reality, and she fell into his arms. When he stumbled, she pulled away, suddenly remembering his injury. "You need medical attention!"

"Yes," he said, but his jaw tensed as he

pulled her back into his arms. "But you need to get out of here, too."

She thought she'd heard him wrong. "What? No! It's over, Noel. We did it. We exposed Stark and his operation. We know who was after me and who killed Daniel. They can't hurt us again." Her heart ached as he shook his head. Did he not love her, after all? Had he said that only in the heat of the moment and now realized that he didn't actually mean it?

Crais appeared at Noel's side, taking his mentee by the arm to help Noel remain upright. "He's correct, Miss Browder. We may have cut off the head of the snake, but you're not out of the woods yet, not while the rest of Stark's black ops team is out there under orders to terminate you. Until they're identified and stopped, they'll continue to follow orders. That's how these kinds of teams work."

"But...I can't." Blood pounded in Yasmine's ears, sending fear surging through her veins worse than when General Stark had pointed a gun at her temple. "Not when we've just found each other again. I thought this was over. I thought when we stopped him—"

Noel's hand slipped behind her head and pulled her toward him, silencing her with a strong, firm kiss full of promise. She felt the love and yearning in the press of his lips against hers, and as he released her, she knew the pain in his eyes reflected the same in her own.

"The director of the FBI and the Secretary of Defense have both promised to guarantee your safety," said Crais. He held up his phone. "I'm on the line right now. We're going to get you out of here. It's not safe. We don't know if there are other operatives loyal to Stark inside the building, but there's a rear exit out of this room that will take us directly to a waiting vehicle."

It was all happening so suddenly. Yasmine felt like her freedom and their victory had been snatched away without warning, and she swayed on her feet.

Noel kept his hand behind her head and pressed his forehead against hers. "I'll come back to you. The FBI will keep you hidden until the danger to you has passed. For your own safety, I probably won't know where you are, but I'm going to find these men, and then I'm going to find you."

"Promise?" Yasmine's voice wavered, but she didn't try to stop the show of emotion. She couldn't. Not this time. She was done being strong.

"I promise we'll be together again." He kissed her softly. "And this time, Yasmine Browder, it's not going to take ten years."

EIGHTEEN

Two months later

Yasmine sat on the oversized couch in the FBI safe house, a cup of vanilla rooibos tea in her hands. She wanted to open the blinds and enjoy the sunshine, but she'd been under strict orders since being relocated here—her third safe house in only eight weeks—not to look through an open window. There'd been no additional attacks against her since General Stark had been taken into custody, but every time she was transferred to a new safe house, she heard whispers of nearby activity. She assumed that the FBI moved her every time one of the black ops men got too close. Regardless of the reason, she was grateful for the efforts the FBI and the Department of Defense were making to keep her safe.

A knock startled her as she took a sip of tea, sending it sloshing against the back of her tongue and scalding the inside of her mouth. Who could be at the door? She knew she wasn't supposed to let anyone inside without FBI approval, but that didn't mean she couldn't look through the peephole to see who was there.

She set down her mug and stood as her phone buzzed on the coffee table. A quick glance at it said she'd received a text message from Crais. You have a visitor, said the text. That was strange. How did Crais know?

She crossed the room to the front door and looked through the peephole—then gasped in surprise. She couldn't unlock and open the door fast enough, suddenly feeling as though she'd stepped inside a dream.

Noel stood on the porch, holding a massive bouquet of gorgeous pink and red hibiscus—the national flower of the Kingdom of Amar—and a large, white box. The scent of cinnamon wafted through the air as he gave her a shy smile. "Can I come in?"

She nodded, all her practiced greetings evaporating like smoke. For two months, she'd thought about this conversation and what she'd say to him if they ever saw each other again.

It had felt like the longest two months of her life.

"Hi," he said, stepping inside.

"Hi." She felt the warmth of a blush creep up her cheeks, followed by a sudden flood of butterflies in her stomach. What was going on? She was a grown woman! She'd dodged bullets and faked her own death, and not once had she felt this nervous. Her only consolation was that he looked just as anxious to be standing in front of her again.

"These are for you," he said after a few moments of silence. He handed her the white box, setting the flowers on top. "I admit that I don't know what kind of flowers you like, so I figured what's inside the box would be a good consolation. Plus, uh, I don't know if you've had any for a while."

She lifted the flowers and set them aside— and gasped in delight as she opened the box. "Cinnamon rolls!"

"I wasn't sure if those were the right thing to bring, or…"

She set down the box and wrapped her arms around him in a grateful hug, blinking back tears. Without hesitation, he returned the embrace and held her tight. The security she felt in his arms brought a sense of home that she hadn't felt for months, and she didn't want to let go—but she also hadn't heard from him since that moment the FBI had dragged her off at the Pentagon, and she didn't want to scare him away if anything had changed.

"It's good to see you," she said. "You look good."

He shook his leg, a goofy grin appearing on his face. "Of course I do. I'm all healed up and come bearing good news."

Her heart leaped. "Really? I could use some."

"Let's sit down." Noel guided her to the couch and they sat at either end, but he scooted closer to her and took her hands. "I wanted to be the one to tell you personally that as of this morning, the last of the black ops soldiers has been located and arrested. The Department of Defense spent weeks interrogating General Stark, and it took an outrageous amount of manpower to find these guys, but it's over. Stark's trial hasn't happened yet, but it's a done deal. There's no one left to come after you."

Yasmine's lips parted, surprise stalling the words on her tongue, but Noel beat her to it.

"You can go home."

She reached out and hugged him again, a quick hug of gratitude, but where she thought she'd find relief, a sudden sense of melancholy rushed in.

Noel cupped the side of her face, rubbing

his thumb lightly across her cheek. "What's wrong? I thought you'd be happy to hear it."

She should have been happy. She knew that. But she couldn't shake the sense that she no longer really had anything to go home to. "Noel, I'm grateful—don't get me wrong, but—"

"The rolls are from Cinnamon Sunrise."

She froze, uncertain if she'd heard him correctly. "What?"

He grinned. "Your aunt and my mother made them. Mina, they've been running your bakery since the day we drove off in my mother's car. The place is a rousing success, and frankly, I'm not sure they're going to want to give it up if you go back."

Laughter bubbled up from inside, and she felt a smooth joy begin to creep back into her spirit. "That's amazing. Auntie Zee…well, I suppose it's fitting. Half of the recipes were hers, anyway." She paused, his final words sinking in. "Wait, what do you mean *if* I go back?"

He shrugged. "I mean, it's up to you."

"But of course I'm going back. Even if they're the ones running the bakery, I'm sure I can find a new apartment and help them out. And you're working in Buffalo, right? So…"

Noel slipped off the couch and knelt on the

floor, leaning over. Yasmine thought he'd bent over to tie his shoe, but when he straightened, he held a dark blue velvet box toward her. "Yasmine, I know we haven't seen each other for a few months, and I know our reunion before that wasn't ideal. I'd always hoped to see you again, and I never expected that it would happen with bullets flying over our heads. But truth be told—"

His voice began to waver. Yasmine held her breath in disbelief.

"Truth be told, the moment you dove across the hood of my car and rolled into the passenger seat, shouting at me to drive, I knew. It didn't matter that we'd spent ten years apart. It took me a while to admit it to myself, but Yasmine, I love you. And I have always loved you. I always *will* love you, if you'll let me. I'll help you open a branch of your bakery in Buffalo, or on the other side of the country, wherever you want, if you'll let me. I don't know where the FBI will take me, but I do know that I want you by my side. I never want to be apart from you again—and certainly not for ten years."

He flipped open the box, revealing a beautiful, sparkling diamond ring. Yasmine gasped as her heart took flight.

"I love you, Yasmine Browder. And I know

you love me. The way I see it, if our childhood love was able to span an entire decade apart, I know that with God's help, we can make anything work. Will you marry me?"

She couldn't help but grin. "A new branch of the bakery, you say? You're willing to help me franchise Cinnamon Sunrise? Sounds like a terrifying challenge, but I can't imagine anyone else I'd want to dive into uncertain danger with." Yasmine laughed and leaned in to give him the kiss she'd waited these past two months for. "So, yes, you ridiculous, incredible man," she said. "I will."

* * * * *

If you enjoyed OUTSIDE THE LAW, look for these other titles by Michelle Karl:

FATAL FREEZE
and
UNKNOWN ENEMY.

Dear Reader,

Thank you so much for coming along with Yasmine and Noel on their whirlwind journey. Both of these characters started out feeling a sense of displacement—they were at the start of new chapters in their lives and not entirely settled into the changes yet. I can't even tell you how many times I've felt like that. When folks ask me, "Where are you from?" I tend to answer with, "Which province? I grew up in four." Yep, my family moved a lot! But each time I entered a new phase of life—and I don't even think a person necessarily needs to move geographical locations to feel this way—that sense of displacement was a God-given learning opportunity. Often a tough one (albeit not tough like bullets and car chases, phew!), but I've learned that home is, well, where you find the ones you love.

I also hope you enjoyed seeing a few familiar faces in this story—if you've read *Fatal Freeze*, you probably recognized the heroic CIA agent Shaun! If you've read *Unknown Enemy*, you probably recognized Chief Black, who helped out Colin and Ginny, as well as a return appearance of the Kingdom of Amar via Yasmine's family background. I hope these little cameos were as much fun for you to read as they were for me to write!

I love hearing from readers. Come hang out with me at michellekarl.com or find me on Twitter, @_MichelleKarl_. Thank you so much for reading *Outside the Law*!

Blessings,
Michelle